The Secret Language of Girls

Also by Frances O'Roark Dowell

The Secret Language of Girls

By Frances O'Roark Dowell

Atheneum Books for Young Readers   New York   London   Toronto   Sydney

ATHENEUM BOOKS FOR YOUNG READERS
An imprint of Simon & Schuster Children's Publishing Division
1230 Avenue of the Americas, New York, NY 10020
Copyright © 2004 by Frances O'Roark Dowell
All rights reserved, including the right of reproduction in whole or
in part in any form.
ATHENEUM BOOKS FOR YOUNG READERS
and colophon are registered trademarks of Simon & Schuster, Inc.
Also available in an Atheneum Books for Young Readers hardcover edition.
Designed by Kristin Smith
The text of this book was set in Lomba.
Manufactured in the United States of America
First Aladdin Paperbacks edition October 2005
28 30 29 27
The Library of Congress has cataloged the hardcover edition as follows:
Dowell, Frances O'Roark.
The secret language of girls / France O'Roark Dowell.
p.cm.
Summary: Marylin and Kate have been friends since nursery school, but when
Marylin becomes a middle school cheerleader and Kate begins to develop other
interests, their relationship is put to the test.
ISBN-13: 978-0-689-84421-8 (hc.)
ISBN-10: 0-689-84421-2 (hc.)
[1. Best friends—Fiction. 2. Friendship—Fiction. 3. Schools—Fiction.]
I. Title.
PZ7.D75455Se 2004
[Fic]—dc22   2003012026
ISBN-13: 978-1-4169-0717-6 (pbk.)
ISBN-10: 1-4169-0717-3 (pbk.)
0416 OFF

For my beautiful nieces,
Hannah Dowell, Kirsten Dowell,
Gabrielle Jonikas, and Elizabeth O'Roark

ACKNOWLEDGMENTS

The author would like to thank the following people
for their encouragement and support: Susan Burke;
Caitlyn Dlouhy; Erin Dlouhy (for making the
friendship bracelet on the cover of the book);
Amy Graham; Virginia Holman; Danielle Hudson;
and Clifton, Jack, and Will Dowell.

what would you trade?

"Do you think bugs have dreams?" Kate asked Marylin, nudging a rock with her foot. A mob of roly-polies scurried toward the sidewalk in a state of panic.

"I don't think bugs even have brains," Marylin said, pulling her knees to her chest so the roly-polies couldn't crawl up her legs. "I wouldn't touch those if I were you," she added. "They might carry really gross diseases."

Too late. Kate was jabbing roly-poly after roly-poly with her finger to get them to curl into tiny balls. She scooped up a bunch of the silvery bugs and watched them roll around in the palm of her hand. "Yum," Kate said. "Want some peas for dinner?"

It was at times like these that Marylin thought Kate still had some growing up to do.

A lightning bug flashed a few feet away from where Marylin and Kate were sitting on the front steps of Kate's house, and then the evening sky dimmed just a notch and suddenly the yard was filled with lightning bugs. According to Marylin's little brother, Petey, when lightning bugs flashed their lights, they were sending signals to each other. *Here I am*, they were saying. *Have I told you lately that I love you?*

Kate was up and running. She swooped like a bird every time a lightning bug flashed in her path, using her cupped palm like a small butterfly net to nab one bug after another. The sky dimmed another notch, and now Kate's tanned legs looked white as paper, as though she'd turned into a ghost. Marylin could see Kate's bare feet glowing like two little moons as she ran through the damp grass.

"Okay, let's see here," Kate said, walking back to the steps, her hands trapping the flashing lights, red glowing through her fingers. She peeked through the small crack between her thumbs. "I count six, no, seven lightning bugs. What would you trade for seven lightning bugs?" she asked Marylin.

What would you trade? It was the game Kate and Marylin had been playing ever since the beginning of nursery school, when Marylin had moved into the house five mailboxes down on the other side of the street. What would you trade for my peanut butter sandwich? My Mickey Mouse ears? For seventeen Pixy Stix?

Marylin dug into her pocket and pulled out half a stick of Juicy Fruit gum. She held it out to Kate.

"No trade," Kate said. "I'm not allowed to chew gum unless it's sugar free."

"That's all I've got," Marylin said. "Take it or leave it."

Kate opened her palms to the humid air and watched the lightning bugs flutter away into the dark. "I guess we shouldn't trade living things, anyway."

The porch light flickered on. Marylin stuck out her leg in front of her and examined her foot. "How about toes? I'd trade toes with you."

Marylin thought her toes were her worst feature. She couldn't believe she had never noticed how weird her toes were until Matthew Sholls had pointed it out to her at the swimming pool the day before. Her second toes were longer than her big toes, and her little toes barely existed. All the rest of her toes were sort of crooked. Kate had perfectly normal, straight toes. Her big toes were the longest, just like they were supposed to be. Kate's little toes were like two plump peanuts.

Kate sat down next to Marylin. "Toes? Who cares about toes?"

Marylin faked a laugh. "Yeah, I know, it's pretty dumb. You're right. Who cares about toes?"

"Come on," Kate said. "Let's go see what's on TV."

Marylin followed Kate inside. The air-conditioning hummed a steady stream of cool air through the house. Marylin shivered a little as she and Kate made their way down the stairs to the basement TV room. She should have brought a sweater with her. She should have brought some socks to cover up her crooked toes.

As much as Marylin hated to, she had to admit it: She was the sort of person who cared about toes.

In three weeks Marylin and Kate would begin sixth grade. The idea of starting middle school made Marylin's stomach go icy cold, like she'd swallowed a cupful of snow. She thought it was possible she would start having boyfriends in sixth grade. A lot of girls she knew had boyfriends. It was a very normal thing to do.

The fact was, Marylin hadn't officially talked to a boy since she'd punched Dale Morrell in the nose in fourth grade. Boys made her nervous, and Marylin preferred to avoid nervous-making situations. But according to the books on puberty her mom had given her last week, any second now she could be chasing Dale Morrell through the hallways of Brenner P. Dunn Middle School trying to make him kiss her. Marylin had known some fifth-grade girls who had done that. Brittany Lamb was practically famous for it. It was the sort of thing Kate couldn't stand. Kate hated kissing of all kinds.

Marylin had mixed opinions about kissing. She liked it when her dad kissed her on the nose at bedtime, but she hated being kissed by Grandma McIntosh, whose kisses left gooey, fuchsia lipstick prints on Marylin's cheek. As for kissing boys, well, Marylin just didn't know. If they were movie stars, sure. Marylin had already spent a lot of time imagining kissing movie stars. But in real life Marylin didn't know any movie stars. She knew boys like Matthew Sholls and Dale Morrell. They were not the kind of people who inspired her to dreams of kissing.

Before going over to Kate's house, Marylin had been sitting on her bed, pulling her left foot as close to her head as possible so she could examine her toes, when her mother had walked into the room and flopped down next to her.

"Mom, do you think my toes would look normal if I put nail polish on them?" Marylin asked. She wiggled her toes so her mom could take in the full effect of their weirdness.

"You have wonderful toes!" Marylin's mom exclaimed. "You have my aunt Bette's toes. Everyone loved Aunt Bette."

"Yeah, but did everyone love her toes?"

"What is this toe obsession of yours, Shnooks?" Marylin's mom put on her I'm-a-concerned-mother-and-I'm-here-to-help face, which Marylin liked a lot better than the leave-me-alone-I've-just-had-a-fight-with-your-father face she'd been wearing earlier in the afternoon, right after Marylin's dad had left on another business trip. Marylin tried not to think about the fight or the trip or the fact that she had to spend the night at Kate's tonight so her mom could call up Aunt Tish and complain about her dad. She'd rather think about toes.

"I don't want to miss out on any of life's big opportunities because of my toes," Marylin explained. "Am I too young for plastic surgery?"

That was when her mom talked to her for a long time about boys and how, no matter what, Marylin was not to pull any stupid beauty stunts to get boys to like her, like bleach her hair platinum blond or pluck off all her eyebrows or get plastic surgery on her toes. And makeup was definitely out. Marylin's mom was famous for being against eleven-year-old girls wearing makeup. It was one of her favorite topics of discussion.

"You're a very pretty girl, Marylin," her mom insisted. "People pay to have hair like yours—it's like moonlight. And brown eyes? Please! Don't ruin what nature's given you."

"But what about nail polish, Mom?" Marylin asked when her mom was through. "Nail polish isn't really makeup."

Her mom considered this for a moment. Ever since she and Marylin's dad had been fighting so much, you could sometimes get her to change her mind about things. It was like she had only so much fighting energy in her. "No black," she said finally, giving Marylin a stern look. "I absolutely forbid black."

"No black," Marylin had promised.

"So when did you start painting your toenails, anyway?" Kate asked Marylin during a commercial break. "I can't believe your mom would let you do that."

"She said it was okay," Marylin said, wiggling her toes so they shimmered a little in the TV's blue glow. "I just can't use black or purple or anything like that. My mom said pink is perfectly respectable."

"Whatever," Kate said, turning back to the TV, where a glamorous woman was shaking her head around so that her hair bounced up and down like a Slinky. The woman was wearing a long, silky dress that was cut low in the front. Watching her made Marylin feel itchy. She wondered what the glamorous woman's parents thought when they saw her on television. Did they wish she'd covered up a little more?

Marylin picked up a pen and a pad of paper from the coffee table. Lately she'd been practicing her signature, trying to make it look more sophisticated. Who knew—maybe she'd be a movie star one day and would have to sign autographs left and right. A few weeks ago she'd changed the spelling of her name from Marilyn to Marylin, to make it seem less old-fashioned. How her parents had come up with the idea of naming a girl born on the very brink of the twenty-first century *Marilyn* was beyond her.

"Who's 'Marylin'?" Kate asked, peering over Marylin's shoulder. "Did you know you were spelling your own name wrong?"

"This is how I spell my name now," Marylin explained. "It's the new me."

"Why do you need to be a new you?" Kate

wanted to know. "There's nothing wrong with the old you. I like the old you."

"I'm sick of the old me," Marylin said. She hadn't realized this until she said it out loud, but she instantly knew it was the truth.

Sounds of distress from the kitchen suddenly tumbled down the stairs. "Scram! Go on now!!" Kate's mom cried. "Get away from there, you dumb cat!"

Kate jumped up. "What's wrong, Mom?" she called, running to the stairs.

"Oh, there's this stupid cat—" Mrs. Faber's voice broke off. Marylin could hear her pounding on the window. "Stop that! Stop that!"

Kate flew up the steps, Marylin following close on her heels. When they reached the kitchen, Mrs. Faber was out in the yard chasing an orange cat with a bird in its mouth.

"Drop it, you stupid animal!" Mrs. Faber yelled after the cat as it disappeared in the dark border of the boxwood shrubs. She turned to Kate and Marylin, who had joined her in the yard. "This is why we have a dog," she said angrily. "Dogs don't eat birds."

"Don't you remember that time Max tried to eat a duck?" Kate asked her mom. Max was the Fabers' basset hound.

"Max wasn't trying to eat the duck," Mrs. Faber said, sounding irritated. "He was trying to smell it. That's what basset hounds do. They smell things."

Marylin heard a peeping noise from the bushes in front of the Fabers' screened porch. She followed the peeps until she found a nest perched on a tight canopy of branches illuminated by the porch light. In the nest was a tiny gray bird with its mouth opened so wide, Marylin could see all the way down its throat.

"It's waiting for its mom to come back to feed it," Kate said, coming up behind Marylin. "It looks really hungry."

"I don't think its mom is coming back," Mrs. Faber said. She patted Kate's shoulder. "I think the cat got its mom."

"I guess we'll have to feed it, then," Kate said. "We'll put its nest in a shoe box and keep it inside, where it can be warm at night. We'll find it some worms."

"It probably won't make it, Kate," Mrs. Faber said. She sounded sad. "I don't think the little bird will make it without its mom."

Kate ignored her mother. Turning to Marylin, she said, "Go get Petey. He can help us dig up worms. Tell him to bring a flashlight. And ask your mom if she has an eyedropper. We'll need an eyedropper."

Marylin felt like a soldier taking orders from General Patton. "Yes, sir!" she said to Kate, and then she turned and ran through the damp grass toward home, wondering when Kate had suddenly become boss of the world.

The lights were on at the new people's house, Marylin noticed as she crossed the street. It used to be the Savoys' house, but then Mr. Savoy got a new job in Boston and Mrs. Savoy decided she'd prefer not to move to Boston with Mr. Savoy. Marylin's mother was on the phone with Mrs. Savoy every day for almost a month, discussing the pros and cons of various apartment complexes around town.

The new people had a girl who was a year older than Marylin and Kate. Her name was Flannery, which Marylin had learned the day before, when she and Kate had gone over to introduce themselves. If Marylin had been the new person on the street, she would have been shy and not said too much, just asked a few questions about school and what kind of clothes everybody wore. Mostly she would have just appreciated two girls coming over to say hi, even if they were only sixth graders and she was a seventh grader. Flannery was not that type of person at all. She'd started bragging immediately how she'd been the most popular person in the history of her old school, and she was sure that everyone in her new school would be really boring.

"Talk about a huge letdown," Kate said as she and Marylin had walked back over to Marylin's house. "I was hoping she'd be a good person to be friends with. And I was especially hoping she'd like basketball, but she is definitely not a team player."

Marylin knew exactly what Kate meant. But at the same time, she'd found Flannery a little bit fascinating, in a scary sort of way. Imagine not caring what people thought about you. Imagine being one hundred percent sure you would automatically be the most amazing person in your class, as Flannery most certainly did.

Marylin tried as hard as she could, but she couldn't even begin to imagine being a girl like Flannery.

The little bird was peeping from its nest in a shoe box on Kate's desk. Marylin struggled out of her sleeping bag and pulled herself up on her elbows to look at the clock radio, which informed her it was 2:13 A.M. She wondered if the little bird would ever fall asleep.

"Maybe it wants another worm," Kate said from her bed, startling Marylin. She hadn't realized Kate was awake.

"You just gave it a worm at midnight," Marylin said. "How many worms can a baby bird eat?"

"How many lawyers does it take to screw in a lightbulb?" Kate answered, giggling.

"What?"

"It's a joke my dad tells," Kate explained. "I don't remember the answer, though."

Marylin sighed. Kate was back in first-grader land. She looked like a little kid just waking up, with her short brown hair sticking out in a million directions, like a tornado had touched down on it for a few seconds. "Maybe you should get some sleep," she told Kate gently.

Kate picked up a flashlight from her bedside table and trained its beam on the shoe box. The little bird's beak glowed red in its light.

"I can't sleep," Kate said. "Someone has to stay up with the bird in case it needs anything." She scootched out of bed and walked over to her desk, where she dipped the eyedropper in a glass of water. "Are you thirsty, little bird? Do you want something to drink?"

Turning to Marylin, Kate said, "We ought to give it a name so we can call it something besides 'little bird.' How about Pee Wee?"

Marylin slid back in her sleeping bag. "It's probably going to die," she said. "I'm not sure naming the bird is a great idea." Then Marylin thought maybe that was a mean thing to say, especially at two fourteen in the morning. Still, it was about time Kate learned the facts of life. It was time that Kate grew up a little bit.

"But maybe it won't die," Kate said, sitting on the floor next to Marylin's sleeping bag. "Remember in second grade when Priscilla Jones got really sick and everyone thought she was going to die? But she didn't. She got well again because she had really good doctors."

"Priscilla Jones wasn't a tiny bird without any mother," Marylin pointed out. "And besides, you're not a doctor."

"But I might be someday," Kate said. "I might grow up to be a vet."

Marylin closed her eyes. When she opened them again, the clock read 4:38 A.M. Kate was sitting at her desk, hovering over the peeping little bird.

"Pee Wee, Pee Wee, Pee Wee," Kate was singing to the little bird. "One day you'll fly through the trees."

When the sun forced Marylin's eyes open the next morning, the first thing she noticed was how quiet Kate's room was. As soon as she saw the shoe box on Kate's desk, Marylin realized why. The little bird had stopped peeping.

Marylin looked around the room as though she expected to see the little bird perched on the windowsill or asleep on Kate's pillow. Instead she saw Kate's feet on Kate's pillow. Kate's head was propped against a stuffed giraffe. She was snoring small, whistling snores.

"Little bird?" Marylin whispered as she worked her way out of the sleeping bag. "Pee Wee?" she whispered as she walked over to Kate's desk. "Are you ready for your breakfast worm?"

The little bird lay very still in its nest. Marylin slowly reached out her finger toward it. She didn't want to scare the little bird. But the little bird didn't move when Marylin touched it. It just lay there, cold and stiff.

"I guess you died," Marylin said to the little bird. "I guess I knew you would."

Marylin sat down in the desk chair. The thing was, she hadn't really known the little bird would die. She had just said it to be mean. Maybe the bird had heard her and lost all hope.

Kate's snores made a soft music from the bed. Marylin thought about waking her up to tell her about the little bird, but she didn't. Instead she sat very quietly and looked at her feet.

She would trade her pink toenails to hear the little bird peep.

"Dearly beloved, we are gathered here today to mourn the loss of a friend who everyone will miss, especially me."

Kate stood over the little bird's shoe box in the backyard, her hands clasped at her waist, a black hat pulled low over her brow. Marylin thought the hat added a respectfully somber note to the proceedings, even if it was from Mr. Faber's Charlie Chaplin costume.

Marylin had been afraid that Kate would start crying that morning when she woke up to find that the little bird had died. But Kate had just stroked the little bird's down a few times and said, "Well, I guess he's with his mom in heaven now. I guess he's probably pretty happy about that."

Then she had thrown on a pair of jeans and her "I'm with Stupid" T-shirt and carried the little bird's shoe box downstairs to the screened porch.

"I'll fix us some cereal while you get dressed," she'd told Marylin after she'd come back inside. "Then we'll plan the funeral."

The funeral procession left the screened

porch for the woods lining Kate's backyard at 11:30 A.M. Kate carried the little bird in its box, followed by Marylin and her brother, Petey. Kate had asked her mom if she wanted to come, but Mrs. Faber said funerals made her sad, and besides, she had to go to work.

"Does anyone have any last words they'd like to say?" Kate asked after her opening remarks. She took off her black hat and held it over her heart.

Petey stepped forward. "I didn't know Pee Wee very well," he said. "But I wish I did. From what everyone says, it sounds like he was really nice."

"Thank you, Petey," Kate said solemnly. She turned to Marylin. "Is there anything you'd like to say?"

Marylin wasn't sure. All morning she had been wrapped in quiet, as though all her words had slipped away from her along with the little bird. Marylin had never known anyone who died before, not even a cat. It made her feel the way she did the day before she got the flu, as though she were floating outside herself. Everything seemed to be happening far off in the distance. The trees shimmered in the late-morning heat, and Marylin wished the little bird's mother had built her nest in one of them instead of a dumb, low-to-the-ground bush.

Marylin decided she didn't like funerals and she especially didn't like things dying.

"That's okay, Marylin," Kate said after a few moments. "Sometimes words don't say what you mean anyway."

Then Kate lowered the little bird's shoe box into the hole she had dug earlier and threw a handful of dirt over it. She motioned for Marylin and Petey to do the same.

"Amen," Kate said, brushing the dirt from her hands.

"Amen," Marylin and Petey echoed her.

Then Petey went home to watch *Mr. Rogers*.

"You want me to show you how to play Parcheesi?" Kate asked Marylin as they walked inside. "My dad taught me the other night. It's pretty fun."

"I don't feel much like playing right now," Marylin said. She really didn't think it was the time for games, anyway. Sometimes it was terrible how insensitive Kate could be.

"Me either, I guess," Kate said. She was quiet for a minute, and then a smile bloomed across her face. "Hey, I know. Let's go to your house and you can show me how to paint my toenails."

Marylin was stunned. "You want to paint your toenails?"

Kate shrugged. "Why not? I think it looks sort of nice. It makes your toes look like little seashells."

That was a funny thing about friends, Marylin thought. You could know a person practically your whole life and she could still surprise you.

"Okay," Marylin said. "Sure. It's not that hard after you practice awhile. It's kind of like learning how to color inside the lines."

Marylin followed Kate out the front door. Birds flew overhead, singing to one another across the wide, blue sky.

"Do you ever think about kissing boys?" Marylin asked suddenly, wondering what other surprises Kate might have tucked away.

"Only movie stars," Kate said. "I would only kiss a boy if he was a movie star."

"Yeah, me too." Marylin nodded, the wind lifting the back of her hair like a wing. "That's exactly how I feel about it too."

attack of the killer hearts

The hearts had been Kate's idea.

"The Three of Hearts? Get it? Like in deck of cards?" she'd prodded Marylin and Flannery, hoping to see the tiniest flicker of interest in their eyes.

"I don't know," Marylin said, looking to Flannery.

"Dumb idea," Flannery said matter-of-factly. Flannery always voiced her opinions as though they were facts you could look up in an encyclopedia.

"No, listen, you guys!" Kate protested. "We

each buy a red T-shirt and paint a glow-in-the-dark heart on it. Together we'd be the Three of Hearts!"

Flannery leaned back against her pillows. Teddy bears were scattered around her like adoring fans.

"Together we'd be the three red T-shirts," she said. "Who wants to go trick-or-treating as a T-shirt? I mean, really, I'm a little old to go trick-or-treating at all, but if I'm going to go, I want to be something good."

"So what's your great idea?" Kate asked. She tried to sound sarcastic, but her voice came out watery, like she was about to come down with a cold.

"I say we go as a valentine," Flannery said. She smiled sweetly at Kate. "See, I don't have anything against hearts. They just have to be the right kind of hearts."

As it turned out, the right kind of hearts were made of stuffed red satin, and Flannery and Marylin would wear them over red body-suits and red tights. Kate, it was decided by Flannery, would be Cupid.

"What's so bad about being Cupid?" her mother asked that night at dinner. "I think Cupid is cute."

"Cupid's fat," Kate's older sister, Tracie, said. "Cherubs are always fat."

"Then maybe you should be Cupid," Kate said.

"Speak for yourself, Chipmunk Cheeks."

Kate's dad threw his napkin down on his plate. "You know, I listen to people argue all day as part of my job. It would be nice to have a little peace and tranquility when I get home."

Kate's dad was the sort of lawyer who tried to get people to settle their differences out of court. Kate thought it was a nice sort of lawyer to be, even if it wasn't the richest kind.

"Come on, Mel, they're just squabbling," said Kate's mom, who was a window designer at a store downtown and worked all day with mannequins. "Kids will be kids, et cetera, et cetera." She took a bite of fettuccine. Kate's dad stood up.

"No one in this family has any idea of what kind of stress I'm under," he said. "Absolutely no idea. I'm stressed out and I'm tired and I'm going upstairs to lie down." With that, he pushed his chair back into place and left the room.

"Mel!" Kate's mom called after him. She followed him into the hallway. Tracie took her plate out to the kitchen.

"I would have made a great heart," Kate said to Max.

Max bobbed his head up and down as though he quite agreed.

When Kate woke up Saturday morning, she wondered if all over the country girls clustered in groups of three, and if the third girl always got stuck with the lousy costume, the last sip from the can of soda, and the comic book no one else wanted to read. She was thinking about starting a revolution for third girls when she grew up. After it was over, the Flannerys of the world would have to go trick-or-treating as Cupid for the rest of their lives.

For now, Kate was the one stuck with finding a bow and arrow. Her dad would probably know how to get archery supplies, but lately it was hard to get a word in edgewise between his yelling and his napping.

Kate grabbed her basketball and dribbled it to Marylin's house. She hoped Flannery wouldn't be there. In fact Kate had begun to secretly hope that Flannery's family would move away soon, even though they'd moved to the neighborhood in August and it was only October now.

It had taken just two months for Flannery to completely disrupt Kate's life. Before Flannery had showed up, Kate and Marylin had been best friends, no questions asked. Now Flannery kept edging her way in, inviting Marylin over to her house without asking Kate, making up secret codes for her and Marylin to write notes in. Kate couldn't figure out why a seventh grader would hang out so much with sixth graders, except to boss them around. Well, she had to admit, you didn't get much bossier than Flannery.

Frankly it was starting to get on Kate's nerves.

Maybe the army would give Flannery's stepdad a promotion and send them overseas, Kate thought as she walked up to Marylin's front door. Then Kate and Marylin could go trick-or-treating as a pair of hearts.

Marylin was sitting in front of the television set with a bowl of popcorn perched on her stomach.

"How's your heart coming along?" Kate asked, sitting down on her basketball and rolling herself toward the TV.

"It's ruining my entire weekend," Marylin said. "My mom's been working on it all morning, and every fifteen minutes she calls me to try on what she's sewed so far."

"I bet it looks great."

Marylin grimaced. "Right now it looks like a fat, red pincushion. I'm beginning to wish we'd done your idea."

Kate rolled off her basketball and plopped onto the floor. "We still could, if you really wanted to."

"Flannery thinks it's dumb," Marylin said, as if that settled the matter.

"So what?" Kate asked. "Two against one. We live in a democracy, remember?"

Marylin seemed to consider this. She stared thoughtfully into her bowl of popcorn and twirled a strand of hair around her finger.

"Flannery's not our boss, you know," Kate said. "We don't have to do everything just because she says so."

Marylin gave Kate a long look and shook her head. "We better go as a valentine," she said. "Petey says you can borrow his bow and arrow if you want."

"Marylin, come try this on!" Marylin's mother called from upstairs.

"Back to the drawing board," Marylin said, standing.

Kate dribbled her basketball back down the street. *Some democracy*, she thought, the ball hitting her foot and careening off of it. Two cardinals startled from the branches of a pine tree, and Kate watched them fly away before running after the basketball, which was headed straight for Mrs. Larch's rose trellis. Mrs. Larch was the sort of person who would call your mom if your basketball knocked over her trellis. She was a very touchy woman.

Kate had just managed to outrun the basketball and scoop it up when the ambulance lights began flashing in her driveway. Then the ambulance backed out onto the street and headed toward her. ƎƆИAˈJUᗺMA was written in big block letters above its bumper.

It must have pulled into the wrong drive-way, Kate told herself. They should really give those ambulance drivers better directions.

"Kate! Katie! Come quick! Something terrible!" Tracie stood on their front porch waving frantically in Kate's direction.

What the heck's wrong with her? Kate thought. And then she dropped her basketball in Mrs. Larch's yard and ran so fast, she thought her heart would explode.

The hospital was filled with pinging noises. There was the ping of the elevator as it stopped on the third floor, and pings that came from behind the high counter of the nurses' station, and the pings pinging on the machine next to Mr. Faber's bed. The machine and Kate's dad were connected by a tangle of wires. Kate was scared to get too close to her dad. She was the sort of person who would trip and cause all the wires to come unattached from her dad's chest. She thought those wires might be what were keeping him alive.

"I'm fine, really I am," Kate's dad was saying to Tracie, who was standing next to his bed and crying so hard, her eyelids had swollen into cherry tomato–size pink puffs. "The doctor says that as far as heart attacks go, mine really wasn't that bad. It was more like a protest than an attack. Honestly, sweetie, there's no reason to cry."

Kate did not cry. A whole gang of tears had gathered behind her eyeballs, but they weren't budging. Kate wished she could cry, just so her dad wouldn't think Tracie loved him more than she did. It seemed to be a law in her life that she cried only when she didn't want to, like last week when Robbie

Ballard had called her "Kate, Kate, the Big Fat Primate" during a game of red rover.

"Maybe we should let your dad rest, girls," Kate's mom said from the doorway. Marylin's mom, Mrs. McIntosh, stood behind her. Mrs. McIntosh had driven Tracie and Kate to the hospital. She still had a few sewing pins stuck in the sleeve of her blouse. Kate wondered if she had finished making Marylin's heart.

"It's the stress that caused it," Kate's mom told Mrs. McIntosh in the hospital cafeteria later. "Stress and not enough exercise. And his family has a history of heart problems. Thank God he doesn't smoke."

Kate swirled her straw around the bottom of her milk-shake cup. Then she sucked on it as hard as she could, pulling up the last few drops of chocolate shake and making a noise like a really small person burping.

"Gross!" Tracie exclaimed. "How can you

make noises like that when Daddy's just had a heart attack?"

Kate shrugged. She didn't see how the two things were connected. What did burping noises have to do with heart attacks? If she drank her shake as quietly as she could, would her dad's heart perk up and beat good as new? If she pulled on her straw really hard so that her milk-shake cup caved in, would the machine her dad was hooked up to start pinging so loudly it would sound like a marching band?

Mrs. McIntosh looked at her watch. "Why don't we go upstairs and say good-bye to your dad," she said to Tracie and Kate. "And then we'll go back to my house and order a pizza."

Kate's mom sighed. "Mel always liked sausage on his pizza. I guess those days are over."

The tears that had been hiding behind Kate's eyeballs began to trickle down her cheeks. Her dad would probably never get to eat another sausage pizza in his life. For some reason, that seemed like the saddest thing Kate had ever heard.

By the time Kate got to school on Monday, everyone in her class knew about her dad's heart attack. She was late because her mom had taken her and Tracie to see their dad in the hospital first thing that morning. The pinging machine and its tangle of wires had been pushed into a corner. Kate's dad was sitting up in his bed eating a low-fat corn muffin when his family came in. On the TV mounted on the wall across from his bed, an interviewer was talking to people who were over a hundred years old.

"That will be me in sixty years," Kate's dad had said cheerfully, pointing to a hundred-and-one-year-old man on the screen who was chopping wood in his backyard.

In sixty years Kate would be seventy-one. She scrunched up her face and looked in the mirror next to the TV, trying to imagine what she would look like then.

"Are you getting sick?" her mom asked her.

"Nope," Kate said. "Just old."

When Kate walked into her classroom, everyone was busy working on their solar-system projects. As soon as they saw her, all the kids in her class stared at Kate as though she were a famous celebrity who had come to visit them. Ms. Cahill came over to Kate as she was taking Pluto and Saturn out of her cubbyhole and patted her on the shoulder.

"You're a very brave girl," Ms. Cahill told Kate.

Kate didn't feel brave. Mostly she just felt like herself, except maybe a little more important. After all, it wasn't every day a person's dad had a heart attack and then made a spectacular recovery. That's what the doctor who had stopped by her dad's room that morning had said. A spectacular recovery.

At morning break, a cluster of kids gathered around Kate and asked her about her dad's heart attack. She told them about seeing the ambulance in her driveway, and how, as the ambulance had passed her on the street, she had seen her dad's hand wave weakly at her from the window. Her dad hadn't really waved, but Kate thought it added a nice dramatic touch to her story. She leaned back against the jungle gym and threw out a bunch of big words like *cardialgia* and *coronary thrombosis*. Everyone looked impressed.

"So I guess this means you're not going trick-or-treating," Flannery said.

Leave it to Flannery to ruin a perfectly good discussion, Kate thought. The kids who had been standing around the jungle gym listening to her trickled off to watch the seventh graders play soccer. Now it was just Kate, Flannery, and Marylin.

"That was really good pizza we had at your house Saturday," Kate told Marylin, ignoring Flannery.

Flannery rolled her eyes. "I know you spent Saturday night at Marylin's house, okay? It's only because your dad had a heart attack, so don't try to make me jealous."

Kate shrugged. Who said anything about trying to make anyone jealous?

"So, are you going trick-or-treating or not?" Flannery demanded.

"Of course I am," Kate said. "My dad's coming home from the hospital tomorrow. Why wouldn't I go trick-or-treating?"

Flannery rolled her eyes again. She was the queen of eyeball rolling. "Well, Marylin's having dinner at my house, so just meet us there at six." Then she turned to Marylin. "Come on. I need to show you something."

Kate watched Flannery and Marylin walk toward the school building. She wondered if there was someone in the army she could call to get Flannery's stepdad transferred. *I hear they need soldiers in Istanbul,* she could say. *And there are a few openings in upper east Romania. At least that's what I read in the paper.*

The idea came to Kate forty-five minutes before she was supposed to meet Marylin and Flannery to go trick-or-treating. She had been sitting on her bed in her leotard and tights trying to figure out what someone dressing up as Cupid was supposed to do with her hair. Kate's hair was brown and straight, and it hung exactly one and a half inches below her ears. It was not Cupid hair—she knew that much. Cupids had short, blond, curly hair like Marcie Grossman's in Kate's reading group.

"I just don't feel like a Cupid," she told

Max, who was lying at the foot of her bed. She could tell from Max's expression that he didn't think she looked like a Cupid either.

Kate looked around her room. She was searching for inspiration. When she saw her red T-shirt, the original red T-shirt that had given her the idea she and Flannery and Marylin should go trick-or-treating as the Three of Hearts, a brand-new idea came into her head. Kate smiled.

A huge, grimacing jack-o'-lantern was perched on the steps outside Flannery's house when Kate got there. She thought it looked a lot like Flannery. Before she rang the doorbell, Kate pulled her coat tighter around herself. The night air was cold, but it smelled good, like leaves and dirt and candles. Wearing the coat had been her dad's idea. You'll catch pneumonia without your coat, he had told her. We've had enough medical emergencies in our family this week. Then he had hugged her and offered a bite of his low-fat granola bar.

Flannery answered the door. She was dressed in her heart costume. Only she looked more like a tomato than a heart. Marylin stood behind her. Her heart was better, even if it was a little lopsided. *I bet that's what my dad's heart looked like after his attack*, Kate thought, looking at Marylin.

"Where's your bow and arrow?" Flannery asked.

"I didn't bring them," Kate said. "I decided not to be Cupid."

"So what are you going as?" Flannery wanted to know. "A coat?"

Flannery's mom walked out from the kitchen with a camera. "Let me take a picture of you guys!" she said. "Kate, how's your dad?"

"He's great," Kate said. "He doesn't have to go back to work for three weeks, so he's in a very good mood."

"Wonderful!" Flannery's mom exclaimed. "Okay, Kate, take off your coat so I can get a picture."

Before Kate took off her coat, she pulled a diamond tiara from the pocket. She had gotten it from Tracie, who had worn it two years before, trick-or-treating as Glenda the Good Witch of the North. Kate didn't think the diamonds were real, but she was very careful with the tiara just the same.

"I don't think Cupid wears a crown," Flannery said. "You have pretty strange ideas about how Cupid should look."

"I told you, I'm not going as Cupid," Kate said, putting the tiara on her head. Then she took off her coat. She was wearing red tights and her red T-shirt, which hung down below her knees. She had drawn a heart with a queen in the middle of it.

"What are you, Kate?" Marylin asked. "A princess?"

Kate smiled. "I am the Queen of Hearts."

"How adorable!" Flannery's mom said.

Flannery rolled her eyes. "That wasn't the plan. You're supposed to be Cupid."

"Sometimes things do not go as planned," Kate told Flannery.

"That's very true," Flannery's mom said. "Okay! Picture time!"

Flannery's mom ushered Kate, Marylin, and Flannery out to the front steps so she could take their picture by the jack-o'-lantern.

"You stand in the middle, Kate," she said. "The queen should always stand in the middle."

Kate edged in between Marylin and Flannery. Then she put an arm around each of their shoulders and squeezed everyone together. She was the Queen of Hearts, after all. Sometimes holding everyone together was just her job.

On the second Wednesday in November Marylin woke up with a stomachache. She always woke up with a stomachache the week before she had a party. Stomachaches were her body's way of reminding Marylin that having a party was a good way to ruin her life.

If it had been up to Marylin, the party would have been at Kate's house. Unfortunately Kate's mom had a law against having sleepovers. Last year, when six girls had stayed over, three of them woke up at 4:00 A.M. with the flu and spent the rest of the night throwing up.

After that it wasn't safe to say the word "sleep-over" around Mrs. Faber.

So now Marylin had four hundred things to worry about. Even though Marylin and Kate were planning the party together, Marylin would be the one responsible if Brittany Lamb and Elyse Cassill got in a pillow fight and kept clobbering each other until Elyse got a headache and started to cry. It would be her fault if Ashley Greer spilled juice on the couch and ruined the upholstery. "Why do you let these things happen?" Marylin's mom would ask her, as if Marylin were boss of the universe and could make everyone behave perfectly all the time.

Tuesday night, just as Marylin was adding carrots to the shopping list for the party so her mom wouldn't lecture her about healthy eating habits, Flannery had called with bad news. Marylin knew it was Flannery even though Flannery didn't bother saying so. Flannery was the sort of person who assumed whomever she called would know it was her.

"Your party is going to be so boring," Flannery said first thing. "Everyone's probably going to fall asleep the minute they get there."

"How can you say that?" Marylin protested. "My mom said that maybe we could rent R movies." That was a lie, but Marylin thought it made her sound like a much older person than she actually was.

Flannery laughed. "It doesn't matter what movies you rent, because I'm not going to be there. Therefore, your party is going to be very boring."

Flannery, it turned out, was going with her family to visit her stepdad's brother in Washington, D.C. "We'll probably go out to eat at a really expensive restaurant," Flannery said. "Who knows, maybe the president will be there."

Marylin doubted it, but she didn't say anything. It was useless to argue with Flannery. Flannery thought she was an expert on everything in the world, including the dining habits of the president of the United States of America.

Besides, Marylin had bigger things to worry about now. Suddenly there was a hole in the party where Flannery would have been. Marylin knew that having an odd number of people at a sleepover was a bad idea. If you had only five girls at a party, someone would end up feeling left out. Around 11:00 P.M. the left-out girl would start crying, and then Marylin's mom would come downstairs and say, "There, there," to the left-out girl and give Marylin a look that said, *Why do you let these things happen?*

When Marylin woke up Wednesday morning, she knew the first thing she had to do was find a sixth girl for her party and fast.

Otherwise she would probably walk around with this stomachache for the rest of her life.

"There is no way I'm spending the night in the same room as Mazie Calloway!"

Marylin steadied herself on her swing. When you were arguing with someone as stubborn as Kate, it was important not to be wobbly.

"I don't see what's so bad about Mazie," Marylin said. "I think she's probably a very nice person when you get to know her."

Kate gave Marylin a long look. "Mazie Calloway is the most conceited person who's ever lived. Just look at her!"

Marylin looked across the playground, where Mazie Calloway was standing with Caitlin Moore and Ruby Santiago, the most popular girls in the sixth grade. They appeared to be examining each other's fingernail polish. All year Marylin had been studying these girls, trying to figure out what made them stand out from other girls like splashes of bright-pink paint against a gray background. She thought it had to do with the way they looked at each other with raised eyebrows and laughed, as though they knew the best secret in the world.

"Okay, if you know so much about people, who do you think we should invite?" Marylin said, feeling irritated. Why did Kate have to make life so difficult?

"Elinor Pritchard," Kate said, kicking up a cloud of dirt with her left foot. "I think she would make a very nice addition."

Elinor Pritchard! Marylin rolled her eyes. Elinor was the sort of person who couldn't string four words together to make a sentence. If she invited Elinor Pritchard, she might as well make everyone eat vegetable stew for dinner. Elinor Pritchard would make it that kind of party.

"The thing is," Marylin said slowly, hoping she could reason with Kate, "we need someone who's kind of fun. But who won't get us into trouble." Marylin's mom didn't have much patience with troublemakers.

Kate swung high into the air. As she flew back, she turned her head toward Marylin and said, "Definitely 'no' to Mazie Calloway, and I guess 'no' to Elinor Pritchard too, if you're going to be stuck-up about it. So who else is there?"

Marylin searched the playground, skimming over a dozen or so unsuitable candidates. Marylin didn't think she was stuck-up, but she did have standards. What was the use of inviting someone like Lacey Terrell, whose only topic of conversation was her dog, to a sleepover? It would be a wasted invitation, in Marylin's opinion.

"How about Kayla Townsend?" Marylin asked, suddenly inspired. Kayla was new that year and seemed a little shy, but she played flute in the band and always wore nice clothes and Mr. Kertzner thumbtacked her papers on the bulletin board in nature studies. Kayla Townsend seemed like a well-rounded sort of person to Marylin. She seemed like the kind of person who wouldn't start crying or throwing up in the middle of the night.

Kate dragged her feet in the dirt to slow down her swing. "Kayla might be okay," she agreed when she came to a stop. "At least she's not Mazie Calloway."

"Or Elinor Pritchard," Marylin replied.

Marylin and Kate smiled at each other. They had been friends since nursery school, and if there was one thing they were good at, it was making compromises. Marylin stretched out her arms and felt a wave of relief flow through her. *Maybe this would be a great party,* she thought. *Maybe this will be the best party I ever have.* Two seconds later she thought of forty new things to worry about, but it had been nice for a second to believe everything would turn out okay.

Petey McIntosh sat on the top bunk and examined a dollar bill with a magnifying glass. His sister had given him the dollar to stay in his room during her sleepover, but Petey thought the picture of George Washington looked a little fishy, like George's mom had just told him they were having liver for dinner. On this particular dollar bill George Washington did not appear the least bit presidential, and Petey couldn't help but wonder if Marylin had given him fake money. Everyone knew what a cheapskate she was. Marylin had allowance money saved up all the way from second grade, but what she was saving it for was a mystery Petey still hadn't solved.

The fact was, even though Petey had read every how-to-be-a-detective book he could find in the school and public libraries, he hadn't had much luck yet cracking a case. His problem was, there just weren't that many mysteries for nine-year-old boys to solve, at least not in his neighborhood. And with the one or two mysteries he had stumbled upon, like the time Marylin had had her watch stolen from her swim club locker, he hadn't been able to track down a culprit, even though he'd spent weeks looking for clues.

But strange things could happen at a sleepover, everybody knew that. Sometimes Petey snuck downstairs after his parents had gone to bed and watched detective shows on TV. On TV people got together all the time for parties at old spooky houses, and someone or something was always disappearing. Petey figured if he was ever going to solve a mystery, tonight was his night, even if his house wasn't all that old or spooky.

He shoved the dollar into his pocket and

grinned. Oh, he'd stay out of the way, all right. But that didn't mean he wouldn't be around. Someone had to keep an eye out for clues, after all.

By four thirty-six on Friday afternoon the house was ready. Kate had come home with Marylin right after school, and together they had cleaned up the basement rec room, put extra soap in the bathroom, prepared two bowls of nacho chips and taken the big jar of nacho cheese junk out of the cupboard and put it by the microwave, and paid Petey a dollar to stay in his room, agreeing that he could come out for two bathroom breaks.

"I think this is going to be a really fun party," Marylin said to Kate at five o'clock as they waited for the guests to show up. "I think we should take a lot of pictures, so when we're old we can look back at what a fun party this was."

"Let's just hope we don't run out of nachos," Kate said.

"Oh, quit being so negative," Marylin told her.

Kayla Townsend was the first person to arrive. "We were supposed to bring sleeping bags?" she asked when she saw Kate's and Marylin's bags piled on the couch.

"It's a sleepover," Kate reminded her, grabbing a handful of chips from a bowl on the table. "So at the end of it everyone goes to sleep. It's sort of like a tradition."

"You don't have to be sarcastic about it," Kayla said. "I just thought maybe there'd be cots or something."

Kate shot Marylin a look that said, *Please remember that inviting this person was your idea.*

"It's no big deal!" Marylin said, trying to sound cheerful. "Kayla can use Petey's sleeping bag. I'm pretty sure it's clean."

"I'm not supposed to use other people's

personal stuff," Kayla said. "It might have germs."

The great sleeping-bag debate was interrupted by Brittany Lamb pounding on the front door. "It's snowing!" she said as she walked in and dropped her bags on the floor. "Maybe we'll be trapped here for the whole weekend. Wouldn't that be great?"

Kayla looked like she might cry. "I have a ballet recital tomorrow at four! I can't get snowed in! I'm the star!"

Fortunately Elyse Cassill knocked on the door before Kayla had a chance to get completely hysterical. Her cute older brother stood behind her. Marylin ran her hand through her hair and put on her best I'm-much-older-than-I-look smile. It was one of her goals in life to make a good impression on Elyse Cassill's older brother.

"What time is this thing over tomorrow?" he asked, sounding like he was in a big hurry to get going.

"Um, I don't know exactly," Marylin said. She wished she could come up with some snappy remark that would make Elyse's brother laugh and maybe ask her out to a movie when she was old enough to date. "Twelve, I guess. Is that okay?"

Elyse's brother ignored her. He grabbed Elyse's arm and said, "You better be ready to go as soon as I get here, jerk, or else you'll have to walk home." Then he turned around and left.

"He's so cute!" Brittany squealed as soon as Marylin closed the door. "You're so lucky to have such a cute brother, Elyse!"

"Ben's a loser," Elyse said matter-of-factly, throwing her sleeping bag on top of the pile.

"I think he's nice," Marylin said, even though Elyse's brother had barely looked at her. Maybe he was shy around girls, Marylin thought. Maybe she should have said something about baseball.

"You think every boy is nice," Kate told her.

"A boy could have seventeen tattoos and a snake wrapped around his neck and you'd think he was nice."

"That's not true!" Marylin exclaimed. Every one knew Marylin was scared to death of snakes.

"What's not true?" Ashley Greer, who had just walked in, asked.

"Everybody's here!" Brittany yelled. "Let's order pizza!" She grabbed a pencil and a piece of paper off the table. "What does everyone want?"

"I think I'm going to be sick."

Kayla was sitting in a chair in the corner of the living room. The rest of the girls turned to look at her.

"You're not going to throw up, are you?" Marylin asked. If Kayla threw up, Marylin's mom would probably make everyone go home.

Kayla shrugged. "I think if I practiced my routine for the recital tomorrow, I'd feel a lot better. But everyone has to watch me, okay? You guys can pretend you're the audience for my recital."

Kate groaned. Marylin gave her a look she hoped would say everything she was thinking. She hoped it would say, *Okay, it's obvious inviting Kayla was a big mistake, but she was not my first pick, remember? Anyway, we're stuck with her, and maybe if we watch her do her dance routine, she'll stop talking about throwing up and then we can get on with the party. If you could not be a big pain in the butt about this, I would really appreciate it.*

Kate appeared to get the message. "Okay, guys, let's watch Kayla dance and then we'll order pizza."

All the girls but Kayla crowded together on the couch.

"You'll really like this," Kayla said, beaming, now that everyone's attention was on her. "Everyone loves to watch me dance."

Elyse Cassill had a fishy look around her eyes, Petey decided, and that brother of hers was definitely up to no good. What did they have planned? Some sort of heist, probably. Was there a black market for sleeping bags? Sure, Petey had watched Elyse's brother drive off in his beat-up old car, but that didn't mean he wouldn't be back later. Petey could just picture Elyse shoving stolen merchandise out the downstairs bathroom window and into her brother's greedy hands.

Oh, he'd be keeping an eye on Elyse Cassill tonight, you could count on it.

Petey could see everything from his spot halfway down the stairs, where he could poke his nose through the railing and nobody would ever notice. He watched that girl Kayla dance. She wasn't a very good dancer, which made Petey suspicious. Maybe she was trying to distract the other girls while Elyse Cassill's brother snuck in the back door and grabbed all their stuff.

Petey eyeballed the rest of the girls. Who

else was involved in this scheme? There was that Brittany girl, who had stolen French fries from Petey at McDonald's once when she thought he wasn't looking. She was a pretty shady character. And one time Ashley had borrowed some socks with cow spots all over them from Marilyn and never given them back.

Overall, it was a crowd you'd be dumb to leave alone with your fancy silverware. Except for Kate. Petey planned on marrying Kate someday, though he hadn't mentioned that fact to her yet. Kate wasn't like other girls. She was reliable and a good basketball player. Petey thought Marylin was dumb to hang out with that bossy Flannery when she could spend all day with Kate if she wanted.

Maybe Petey should write Kate a note to let her know that something suspicious was going on down there, right underneath her nose. He'd hate to see her become a victim of a crime. He tiptoed up to his room for a sheet of paper and a pencil. But as soon as he opened his door, he heard it: the sound of a dilapidated car engine, the very sort you'd find in Elyse Cassill's brother's car, puttering on the street outside his window. He turned out the light and climbed onto the top bunk, his binoculars in hand.

The plot, he was pretty sure, had thickened.

After they finished eating pizza, braided one another's hair, and watched *Ghost* twice, the girls decided to hold a séance and see if the spirit of Marilyn Monroe had anything to say to them.

"Are you here among us, Marilyn Monroe?" Kate asked in her spookiest voice, the one she reserved for séances and ghost stories. "Give us a sign, O great movie star."

The thump from overhead was loud and clear.

"That was not Marilyn Monroe," Marylin

said, trying to stop everyone from screaming. "That was Petey falling out of bed. He does it all the time."

"That didn't sound like a body-falling-out-of-a-bed sort of thump to me," Ashley said. "It was a lot more like a spirit trying to contact us from the other side. It was exactly that sort of thump!"

Elyse Cassill started to cry. "I hate séances! They're so dumb!"

Brittany handed Elyse a Hershey's with almonds. "Eat some chocolate, Elyse. You'll feel a lot better."

"Ssh!" Kate said in a loud whisper. "I hear something. Maybe Marilyn Monroe is in the room with us."

The basement door burst open, which made everyone scream at the top of their lungs. Elyse jumped into Brittany's lap.

"It's only me!" Marylin's mother called. "I wanted to let you know that the noise you probably heard was Petey falling out of bed. What on Earth are you girls up to?"

"Nothing, Mrs. McIntosh," Ashley said in the voice she used to butter up parents. "Just telling ghost stories. Elyse got a little carried away."

"I did not!" Elyse shouted through her sobbing.

"It's time to go to sleep, guys," Marylin's mom said firmly. "It's past midnight. No more ghost stories, okay?"

Marylin went to the laundry room to get Petey's newly germ-free sleeping bag out of the dryer. She wondered if she should spray it with Lysol so it would smell especially disinfected. Who would have guessed that Kayla Townsend would be the sort of girl who worried about germs? Marylin's mom was always saying you shouldn't judge people by appearances, and Marylin was beginning to think that maybe she was right. Maybe they should have invited Elinor Pritchard after all.

When Marylin got back into the rec room, the other girls were rolling out their sleeping bags and arguing over who would sleep next to whom.

"I'm sleeping next to Marylin," Ashley said in a bossy voice.

"I want to sleep next to Marylin too!" Elyse yelled. "I get to be on her other side!"

Marylin handed Kayla Petey's sleeping bag. "Where do you want to sleep?" she asked.

"I need to sleep in the middle of everyone," Kayla said. "If my legs get cold, I won't be able to dance my best tomorrow."

"We could all pile up on top of you," Brittany offered sweetly.

Kate came to the rescue. "Okay, here's how it's going to be," she said in her army-general voice. "Ashley, Marylin, and Elyse, line up your sleeping bags next to each other. Then Kayla, you put your sleeping bag so it runs across the end of Ashley, Marylin, and Elyse's. Then Brittany and I will put our sleeping bags next to yours. Then everyone can live happily ever after."

"I don't want to sleep at people's feet," Kayla complained. "Marylin, you guys put your sleeping bags so your heads are at my side."

Ashley started to protest but then thought better of it and did as she was told.

When all the sleeping bags were rolled out, they formed a squished T. The girls slid into their bags and rustled around until they were comfortable. Elyse let out a big yawn and said, "I'm pooped."

Kayla sat up. "I'm not," she said. "I'm bored. Let's do something! Where's the phone?"

"There's one in the kitchen," Marylin said. "But I don't think it's such a great idea to make any calls. My mom would probably hear you."

Later, when Marylin thought things over, she would realize that it was at this point the party started to spiral completely out of her control.

Ashley sat up. "I know a great prank phone call we could do!"

Kayla grabbed Ashley's hand. "Come on! Let's go call someone! Let's call Robbie Ballard!"

Robbie Ballard was the cutest boy in the sixth grade. Well, Marylin thought, at least Kayla has good taste.

Kayla and Ashley rumbled up the stairs to the kitchen, leaving Marylin, Kate, Elyse, and Brittany to stare at one another.

"You're probably going to get in big trouble for this," Elyse said, sounding sympathetic.

"Yeah," Kate agreed sadly. "Your mom has ears like an elephant."

"Whose idea was it to invite Kayla, anyway?" Brittany asked.

Marylin and Kate looked at each other. "Both of ours," Kate said, patting Marylin's shoulder. "It seemed like a good idea at the time."

Ashley's and Kayla's giggles filtered down

from the kitchen. Marylin could hear them making loud *sshh*ing noises at each other. It was only a matter of moments before Marylin's mom would descend the staircase and ground Marylin for life.

Marylin stood up. It was time to let something happen. "Everybody get dressed!"

"Get dressed?" Elyse look confused. "I just put on my nightgown. Besides, we're supposed to be asleep."

Marylin began pulling on her jeans over her pajamas. "That's right, we're supposed to be asleep, but we're not. And in a few minutes my mom will come downstairs and find those guys in the kitchen making prank calls and we'll all get in trouble."

Everyone nodded. That was a rule when it came to sleepovers. If the mom in charge got mad at one person, she got mad at all of them. It saved a lot of time in the long run.

"Well, if we're all going to get in trouble anyway," Marylin said, wiggling her head through the neck of her sweater, "we might as well get in trouble for something good."

Petey tried to roll over, but he was trapped. Elyse Cassill's older brother! How had he gotten into Petey's room? Petey wrestled with all his strength, but his arms were pinned to the bed. "Get off of me, you jerk!" he cried. "Don't think you're going to get away with this!"

The bedroom door opened, light from the hallway flooding in. "What's all this yelling?" Petey's mom stood in the doorway. She did not look like a mom who was concerned that her son was fighting for his life. She looked like a mom who was seriously annoyed. She walked over to the top bunk and yanked at Petey's sheets.

"You're having a dream and you're all tangled up in your sheets," she told him. "One minute you're falling out of bed, the next minute you're being choked to death by your sheets. I should make you sleep on the couch."

Suddenly something outside Petey's window caught his mom's attention. Elyse Cassill's brother! Petey knew it! "He's been there all night, Mom," Petey informed her. "Just waiting for his chance."

Petey's mom struggled to open the window, then gave up. "Get in bed, Petey, and stay there," she said, stomping out of the room.

"But I am in bed," Petey called after her, jumping down from the top bunk. He grabbed his binoculars and peered out the window. Where was that scoundrel? At last, the jig was up, thanks to Petey. Even if Elyse Cassill's brother managed to make a getaway, Petey had already ID'ed him. He wondered if the police department would offer him a job as a junior detective.

Petey didn't see Elyse Cassill's brother anywhere. He'd gotten away! But there were Marylin and Kate, plus Elyse and Brittany, standing in the middle of the McIntoshes' snowy front yard. Marylin and Kate were leaning toward each other, whispering.

Petey smiled. He couldn't be happy about the heinous crime, whatever it was, committed here tonight by Elyse Cassill and her brother and the rest of that shady crew, but he was happy to see his sister and Kate best friends again. He sat down on the lower bunk, his eyes growing heavy. Detective work sure could take it out of you, he thought, leaning back against the pillow. "Call me when the police get here," he said, or at least he thought he said it. He was too busy running down his street after some guy whose arms were full of sleeping bags to be sure.

The snow blanketing the front yard made Marylin think of vanilla frosting. She scooped some up with her bare hand and licked it. The snow tasted sweet and fresh and made

Marylin's tongue tingle. She wondered if Eskimos ate snow for dessert. They could pour chocolate syrup on it and it would almost be like having a sundae.

"Marylin, what are we doing out here?" Elyse asked, rubbing her hands together. Behind her the trees held out their frozen branches as though they were asking each other to dance.

Marylin turned to Kate and flapped her arms. She was sending a secret signal that only Kate would understand.

"Snow angels!" Kate yelled.

The four girls stood in a row with a few feet between each of them. "Okay," Marylin instructed. "On the count of three: one, two, . . . three!"

Everyone flopped backward into the snow. Arms and legs scissored in frozen jumping jacks. Overhead the stars flickered and flamed.

When they stood up, four silvery angels were spread across the yard.

"Marylin, what are you girls doing?" Marylin's mom stood at the front door, her robe wrapped tightly around her. Ashley and Kayla peeked out from behind her shoulders.

"Come and look, Mrs. McIntosh!" Kate yelled. "It's like heaven out here!"

"It's freezing!" Marylin's mom ducked back inside. A few moments later she returned to the doorway wearing rubber boots.

"What is all the commotion about?" she asked, trudging through the snow toward the girls. She sounded annoyed. "I find two of you on the phone asking someone if he's got Dr Pepper in a can, and the rest of you are outside catching pneumonia. Marylin, I just don't know why you let these things happen."

"Look, Mom," Marylin said. "Just look."

Her mom looked at the snow and didn't say anything for a second. "Snow angels," she said finally, making the words sound like the beginning of a song. "Your aunt Tish and I used to love to make snow angels." Marylin's mom flapped her arms, as though she could make an angel in the air.

"Go ahead, Mrs. McIntosh," Brittany said. "We'll do it with you."

Marylin's mom nodded her head. "It would be nice to have a yard full of angels."

For the next week, until the snow melted completely and ran in rivulets to the street, the angels stayed stretched out across Marylin's lawn. Every time she walked down her driveway, Marylin thought it was pretty the way the angels melted a little bit every day so that by the end of the week their wings were touching, as if the angels were holding one another up. Her mom's angel was the tallest, and Marylin's angel was right next to it, and Kate's next to Marylin's. Marylin could see the marks in the snow where their arms had flapped and flapped, as though any second they expected to fly.

talk to me

The afternoon sun streamed through the window, making a puddle of light on the kitchen floor. Kate watched it for several minutes, wondering where light went once it got dark outside. Did it fly off to outer space, or did it just stop existing? And did light really have a speed? How could anyone tell? It looked like it was just sitting there to Kate.

Kate walked over to the refrigerator and opened the freezer compartment. Who needed Marylin and Flannery when life was full of interesting scientific mysteries? Who needed friends when you could have a milk shake? Kate decided that she absolutely did not care that Marylin and Flannery were ignoring her, as though she were a pocket of air taking up space on the school bus. It had happened so quickly, without any warning. There had been the party, where everything was like old times—Kate and Marylin, Marylin and Kate. And then Flannery had come back from her trip to Washington, D.C., and a week later no one was talking to Kate anymore.

"You are going to blow up like a balloon if you eat ice cream all the time," Tracie said, walking into the kitchen, where Kate was scooping some Rocky Road into the blender.

"Is that what happened to you?" Kate asked. "Is that your excuse?"

"Oh, please," Tracie said. She opened the refrigerator and took out a can of diet soda. "I weigh exactly what I'm supposed to for my age and height."

Tracie was fourteen and acted like she'd recently been crowned Queen of the Universe. She spent two hours a day in the bathroom glopping makeup on her face and spritzing styling gunk all over her hair. It was a wonder Kate ever got a chance to brush her teeth. She'd probably have a mouth full of cavities next time she went to the dentist, just because Tracie couldn't leave the house without looking like a movie star.

Kate pushed the MIX button on the blender. "It must be a real pain, being so perfect all the time," she told Tracie.

"It can be," Tracie said. "But I do my best to live with it."

Kate pushed the PURÉE button so she wouldn't have to hear anything else that Tracie said for the next thirty seconds. She watched as the fudge and nuts and marshmallows blurred together into one beautiful shade of chocolate brown.

Tracie sat down at the kitchen table and leafed through a fashion magazine. "So why aren't you at Marylin's?" she asked. "Last time I checked, you were practically living over there."

"Marylin's boring," Kate said, pouring her milk shake into a glass. "She never wants to do anything good anymore."

"Or maybe she just doesn't want to do anything with you," Tracie said. "I can't say that I blame her."

It occurred to Kate that throwing her milk shake at Tracie would be a very satisfying thing to do right at that moment. Unfortunately she'd used up the last of the ice cream, and she'd hate to waste perfectly good Rocky Road on someone as dumb as her sister.

"I'll forget that you said that," Kate told Tracie on her way out of the kitchen. "I know you'll feel very horrible about it later, and that's enough for me."

Tracie's gulping laughter followed Kate out the front door to the porch. It was the story of Kate's life. She had friends who didn't act like friends and a sister who didn't act like a sister. Maybe everyone she knew should watch more TV so they could get an idea of how normal people treated each other.

Kate sat down on the top of the steps and began drinking her milk shake. Her next-door neighbor Courtney was standing in her front yard. Courtney was six, and she thought everything Kate did was terrific. Kate could dump a bucket of mud over her head and run in circles around her yard, and Courtney would say, *I want to do that! Show me how to do that!*

"Kate, look what I found!" Courtney yelled. From a distance, in her bright-green jacket, Courtney looked like a giant frog. Kate was amazed that little kids never seemed to care about what they wore. Once she had seen

Courtney walk down the hall at school dressed in ballet slippers, overalls, and a sweater wrapped around her head like a turban. Courtney appeared to have no idea that at that moment she looked like the weirdest person in the world.

"Look what I found with my stick!" Courtney called again. A dingy white piece of fabric was waving from the top of Courtney's stick like a flag. When Courtney got closer, Kate realized it was a dirty sock.

"That's gross," Kate said. "What in the world do you want that for?"

"It's a clue," Courtney said. "I think it's a murderer's sock."

"Why would a murderer's sock be in your front yard?"

Courtney thought about this for a moment. "Because it fell off of him when he was running away."

"Courtney," Kate said, sighing very loudly to

emphasize the fact that she was starting to get annoyed, "what makes you think there's a murderer around here?"

Courtney smiled. "Buddy told me."

Buddy was Courtney's invisible friend. According to Courtney, Buddy never slept, and he could sneak into people's houses without them knowing, and sometimes he had lunch with the president. Courtney always relied on Buddy for the inside scoop.

"Whatever," Kate said, draining the last drop of her milk shake. "I've got to go in now." She stood up and turned toward the front door. Just because her so-called friends no longer spoke to her didn't mean Kate was going to make a habit of hanging out with six-year-olds.

"But, Kate!" Courtney said, running over to the bottom of the steps. "What if the murderer comes back tonight looking for his sock? He could go into your house and kill you!"

"I'll make sure Max sleeps on the end of my

bed," Kate said, not bothering to turn around. "Okay?"

"I don't know, Kate," Courtney said, sounding worried. "I think I better come over and spend the night with you, just in case something bad might happen."

Courtney's big dream was that one day she would be invited to spend the night at Kate's house. She was always inventing excuses about why it was very important that she sleep over. Last week she claimed her mom had a cold, and if Courtney didn't spend the night at Kate's, she would probably catch her mom's cold and die.

"If the murderer kills me in my sleep tonight, you can have all my Barbies, okay?"

"Can I have the Dream House, too?" Courtney asked, sounding excited. Then she must have realized that if Kate got murdered, she wouldn't live next door anymore. "You know what? I don't think there really is a murderer," she called after Kate. "I think Buddy was making that up."

Kate slammed the front door behind her. She wondered which was worse—an invisible friend who made up stories about murderers coming to get you, or real friends who stopped talking to you. Not that she cared, really. She was sick and tired of Marylin and Flannery. She didn't want a thing to do with either of them.

On Thursday morning Marylin and Flannery had officially been ignoring Kate for three days.

It all started when Kate went to the bus stop in front of Flannery's house Monday morning. She said hi, the way she always did, the cold December air turning her breath into a cartoon bubble, but Marylin and Flannery didn't say anything back. Kate tried a few more times to get Marylin and Flannery to say something, but they wouldn't. Kate almost turned around and went home. She suddenly felt like she had a temperature.

Instead she got on the bus and took a seat behind her two so-called friends. She leaned forward and asked, "Did I do something that made you mad? Is that why you're not talking to me?"

Marylin and Flannery looked at each other and rolled their eyes. Flannery leaned over and whispered something into Marylin's ear. Then they both started laughing hysterically.

"Go ahead and be that way," Kate said, sitting back in her seat. "It just shows how immature you are."

"I'd rather be immature than be a certain unnamed person who smells like they haven't had a bath in three months," Flannery said, without turning around.

Kate put her chin to her chest and sniffed. She couldn't smell anything bad. All she could smell was the laundry detergent her mom used.

She sniffed to her left and sniffed to her right. "There is nothing wrong with the way I smell," she said.

This made Marylin and Flannery laugh even harder. Kate felt like she'd been punched in the stomach. She looked out the window and worked very hard not to blink. She wasn't in the mood to cry.

Marylin and Flannery kept ignoring Kate all day. Kate made the mistake of following them to Marylin's house after school, thinking there was some way she could make them talk to her. She thought she might be able to reason with them. Kate was a very reasonable person after all, and until recently Marylin had practically been the most reasonable person on the face of the planet. They should be able to talk things out, shouldn't they? That's what happened when friends had problems on TV. They communicated with each other. Kate and Flannery and Marylin just needed to communicate.

As it turned out, Marylin and Flannery were not in the mood to communicate that afternoon. They let Kate follow them into the house and upstairs to Marylin's room, but whenever Kate tried to talk to them, they acted like she wasn't even there. Kate sat with her back against Marylin's purple love seat, which Kate had helped Marylin pick out at the furniture store the year before. Marylin and Flannery sat on Marylin's bed and talked in especially loud voices, as if they wanted to make sure that Kate wasn't missing a word, even though she was sitting only five feet away.

"You don't have to yell," Kate said after a few minutes. "It makes you sound ridiculous."

Flannery looked around the room. "Did the wind just blow through here?" she asked Marylin.

Marylin giggled. "I think I felt a little breeze, now that you mention it."

Kate stood up. "You are acting like children," she told them, sounding exactly like her mother when she yelled at Kate and Tracie for fighting. "You think this hurts my feelings, but it doesn't."

"Blow, wind, blow!" Flannery said, falling backward as though she'd been hit by a tornado. Marylin flopped against her pillows, shrieking with laughter.

Kate shook her head. To think she had been happy when Flannery had moved into their neighborhood. To think she had turned to Marylin and said, "I hope they have a girl our age," when they saw a family moving into the Savoys' old house a month before school started.

"I have no idea why you're doing this," Kate said, her last effort at getting some response before she left in defeat. "I have absolutely no idea."

Marylin rolled over and looked at Kate. For

a tiny second Kate thought she saw panic in Marylin's eyes.

It occurred to Kate that Marylin had no idea why she was doing this either.

By Thursday Kate was used to Marylin and Flannery ignoring her, which is why it didn't bother her at all anymore. After three days she was practically a professional when it came to being ignored. Kate picked up her lunch from the counter, grabbed her backpack, and went out the front door. *So what if no one talks to me?* she thought as she walked up the street. She'd rather read a book anyway. Talking to people was a complete waste of time, in Kate's opinion.

"Max is following you!" Courtney yelled at her, running across her front yard, her Pocahantas lunch box thumping against her leg. "Are you taking Max to school with you, Kate? Because he's following you!"

Kate looked over her shoulder. Sure

enough, Max was lumbering up the road behind her. Kate sighed. Max was not the sort of dog you could just order to go home. Max never obeyed orders. He'd flunked out of dog school because he never did anything he was told. He was also not the sort of dog you could let follow you to the bus stop. You never knew when Max would decide to lie down in the middle of the road and take a nap.

Kate turned around and stomped toward Max, grabbing him by the collar when she reached him. She pulled him to her house, muttering under her breath about stupid dogs and the stupid things they did. Max gave her an innocent look.

By the time Kate had shoved Max into the house and headed back for the road, she could see that the bus had reached the stop in front of Flannery's house. Now Kate would have to stand at the edge of her own driveway and get on the bus with Courtney, who went to the elementary school next door to Kate's middle school. They should not put elementary school kids and middle school students on the same bus, in Kate's opinion, especially since Kate's getting on the bus with Courtney would give Flannery the opportunity to say loud enough for everyone to hear, "Don't the first graders look cute today?"

"Kate, Kate, look at this!" Courtney said, sliding in next to Kate on the sticky bus seat. Courtney held out a piece of paper with a drawing of something Kate didn't recognize.

"It's a horse!" Courtney exclaimed proudly. "I think it looks really good, don't you?"

Kate nodded in a way she hoped would suggest to Courtney she was not in the mood for talking. But Courtney never picked up on Kate's subtle hints.

"I think I'm going to draw two hundred horses," Courtney said, "and then hang them up in my bedroom like wallpaper. You could help me, Kate. You draw the best horses."

Kate gave up. "Here, give me that," she told Courtney, grabbing the piece of paper. "If you're going to draw horses, you have to know how to do their noses right. This looks more like a dog than a horse."

"It's a good horse," Courtney said, pouting. "My mom said it's the best horse she's ever seen in her life." She grabbed the paper from Kate. "Give me my horse!"

"Fine," Kate said. She turned her face to the window. From behind her came Flannery's squawk of laughter.

Courtney turned around in her seat. "Don't laugh, Flannery, you squirrel butt! I bet Kate can draw horses a lot better than you can!"

My hero, Kate thought.

When she walked into her homeroom, Kate saw that Ms. Cahill had written her name along with Elinor Pritchard's and Doug Brezinski's on the board. *Ms. Cahill's Poetry*

$\mathcal{S}$tudents was written above their names in the teacher's flowery cursive.

"I've chosen you three to do something special," Ms. Cahill told Kate, Elinor, and Doug after she called them into the hallway. "Because you are my very good writers, you're going to spend two mornings in the library with a visiting poet, along with the other very good writers from the other sixth-grade homerooms."

Kate had never met a poet before. She imagined a man with a white beard who wore a tweed jacket and smoked a pipe, and who would ask them to make a list of words that rhymed with "ocean." *Motion*, Kate thought as she walked to the library. *Lotion, notion, potion.*

To Kate's surprise the visiting poet turned out to be a woman with wild red hair that fanned out from her head like a forest fire. Giant purple earrings in the shape of seashells dangled from her ears. They matched her gauzy purple skirt and her purple cowboy boots.

"Hello. I'm Sara Catherine Toole," she introduced herself to Kate, Elinor, and Doug. Sara Catherine Toole's voice didn't match her outfit at all. Her voice was serious and down-to-earth, as though she thought it was very important that the children knew her full name.

The other very good writers from the sixth grade trickled into the library. Kate's stomach jitterbugged when she saw Marylin. It was the first time in three days she and Marylin had been together in a room without Flannery standing by Marylin's side and jabbing Marylin with her elbow practically every time Kate moved a muscle. Maybe this would be Kate's opportunity to make Marylin talk to her. Maybe poetry would bring them back together.

Not that Kate cared.

As soon as Sara Catherine Toole asked

everyone to sit down, Kate grabbed the chair next to Marylin. Marylin looked around quickly, as if to see if there were another seat she could take, but it was too late. There were nine chairs for nine students, and all of them were filled.

"This is going to be fun, don't you think?" Kate asked Marylin, trying to sound like everything was normal between them.

Marylin looked straight ahead. "I can't talk to you," she whispered.

"Why not?" Kate asked. "Other kids are still talking."

"I mean I'm not allowed to talk to you. And I have to report everything you say, so just be quiet, okay?"

Marylin didn't sound like she was mad at Kate. She sounded like she was trying to protect Kate from something more powerful than the two of them put together.

"Okay, everyone. We're going to start out with some free writing to get your creative juices flowing," Sara Catherine Toole announced from the head of the table. "I'm going to give you a phrase, and you'll have two minutes to write everything that comes to your mind about that phrase, okay? The first phrase I want you to free write on is 'Best Friend.'" Sara Catherine Toole checked her watch. "Ready? One, two, three, go!"

After a minute Kate glanced over at Marylin, who had started writing immediately. "Best Friend" was printed across the top of her paper. And right beneath that, in very small letters, Marylin had written "Squirrel Butt."

Kate had discovered that lunch was the worst time of the day if your so-called friends were ignoring you. She had tried reading a book while she ate her sandwich, but she got too caught up in the story. Twice that week she hadn't heard the rest of her class get up and go outside to the playground after everyone was done eating. It had been very embarrassing to look up and realize she was the only person from Ms. Cahill's class left in the cafeteria.

On Thursday Kate ate her sandwich as fast as she could and then got permission to go to the library. She had decided to look for books about people who got ignored by their friends. Maybe some famous author had been ignored by her best friend when she was a kid and had some interesting opinions on the subject.

She found three books on friendship, but they were no help at all. One of them was called *A Friend Is . . .* , by Margie Majors-Reinholdt. Every page had "A Friend Is . . ." at the top, a picture of two girls picking flowers or baking cookies in the middle, and at the bottom a sentence like "Someone who cheers you up" or "Someone who cares about you." *A Friend Is . . .* , by Margie Majors-Reinhold, made Kate want to throw up.

Kate flipped through the encyclopedia and the dictionary, but neither of them had anything to say about being ignored, so she started roaming at random through the shelves. She found a good book on famous Olympic athletes, and another on rainy-day activities such as making a phone with two cans and a piece of wire that looked pretty interesting, but nothing on friends who suddenly act like you're the dumbest, smelliest person who ever lived.

It really was enough to make a person feel tired, Kate thought as she sat down at a long table by the window. For one thing, being ignored was not exactly a private matter. At home it was just Marylin, Flannery, and Kate, but when you brought your life to school, it started to spread out to other people. So now Brittany and Ashley were acting weird around her, and today during P.E., when she and Elyse were waiting in line to take their turns at the broad-jump pit, Elyse had leaned over to her and said in a low voice, "You know, it might help if you got your ears pierced."

Kate had pulled at her left earlobe. "What would getting my ears pierced help?"

Elyse shrugged. "Your image. You'd seem more mature if you wore earrings. And makeup. At least fingernail polish."

Elyse sounded as though she represented a committee that had spent hours in meetings deciding on how Kate could improve herself.

"I'm not allowed to get my ears pierced until I'm twelve," Kate said. By this time they were at the head of the line, and Elyse had started doing deep knee bends to warm up. "Besides, I'm not really the jewelry type."

"That's too bad," Elyse said, turning to make her jump. "Because people really respect pierced ears."

Kate had a hard time believing Flannery and Marylin were ignoring her just because she didn't have two minuscule holes poked into her head like they did. What kind of people would stop talking to you over dumb stuff like that? She thought about how she and Marylin had practically spent their whole lives together. How could you be best friends with someone forever and then stop talking to them? Had Marylin forgotten the time last summer when her parents wouldn't stop fighting and she'd spent three nights in a row over at Kate's house, no questions asked?

Kate looked around the library, feeling like a detective in search of clues that would unravel a great mystery. Unfortunately from what Kate could tell, the library did not come equipped to help you find the answers to the really important questions in life. All this library had was one measly computer, a card catalogue, and a bunch of tables where all the kids who didn't have friends sat after they finished eating lunch. Which would explain what Elinor Pritchard was doing there.

Kate still remembered how Elinor had carried her lunch to kindergarten in a briefcase instead of a lunch box like everybody else. Kate didn't understand why kids like Elinor never figured out that there was a certain way to act and talk and dress if you wanted to have lots of friends, and that it was practically a law that you would never have friends if you carried your lunch to school in a briefcase. Why couldn't kids like Elinor see that?

Elinor looked up from her table and smiled at Kate. Kate gave her a little wave and was about to leave the library when she was struck by a thought. What if she was turning into Elinor Pritchard? What if that was why Marylin and Flannery were giving her the silent treatment? She looked at what she was wearing to assure herself that she looked like everyone else, which she did. She carried her lunch in a brown paper bag, so that couldn't be the problem.

I am not weird, Kate thought. *I am just myself.* And then Kate wondered if that was what Elinor Pritchard said to herself every morning before coming to school, where most of the kids never said a word to her.

Kate walked over to Elinor's table. "Have you written the world's greatest poem yet?"

Elinor looked down at her notebook and shook her head no.

"Come on," Kate said, nodding toward the library exit. "Let's go to the cafeteria and get some ice cream. Maybe it will inspire you."

Kate sat at the kitchen table, eating graham crackers and looking over the poems she had written the second day in the library with the visiting poet. She wished she had made a copy of her poem that Sara Catherine Toole had chosen to put on the library bulletin board. It was about friends who sometimes didn't get along for reasons no one could figure out. Kate had called it "Talk to Me."

"Listen to this line," Sara Catherine Toole had said to the nine very good writers of the sixth grade after they'd handed in their poems. "'A friend is someone whose face you can see in the dark.' That's beautiful! Can anyone besides Kate tell me what that means?"

Elinor Pritchard raised her hand. "I think it means that if someone's really your friend, they're always with you, no matter if you can see them or if they're even in the same room with you," she offered shyly.

"Wonderful!" Sara Catherine Toole exclaimed. She held up Kate's poem. "We have a real poet here, folks."

A real poet. Kate had tasted those words all the way home on the bus. That's what Sara Catherine Toole said poets did—they tasted words.

Someone tapped on the kitchen door. When Kate went to open it, she found Courtney in her green frog jacket holding the same sock she'd found two days before.

"Buddy told me whose sock this really is," Courtney said, walking inside and taking a graham cracker from the box. "You want to know whose?"

"Sure," Kate said, sitting back down. "Why not?"

"Santa Claus!" Courtney said, practically falling down from excitement. "Buddy saw him last Christmas Eve! You know what else Buddy told me? He said that Rudolph isn't really one of Santa's reindeers. That's just on TV."

"Really?" Kate said. She laughed. "What else does Buddy know about Santa Claus?"

"Well," Courtney said, her face scrunched up with the effort of coming up with a good story, "there's lots of things he knows."

Kate leaned back in her chair. She was ready to let Courtney talk as long as she wanted. She was in the mood to be nice to everyone, even her annoying six-year-old neighbor and Buddy, the invisible friend.

"That was a good poem," Marylin had said to her that morning as they'd left the library for lunch. Five small words followed by a hint of a smile.

Five small words. Kate could taste them.

She was pretty sure there would be more.

why look at the moon?

The day Marylin fell in love with Mr. Kertzner, her nature studies teacher, she decided the only person she would tell was Aunt Tish, who was staying at Marylin's house to recuperate after her divorce from Uncle Nick. Marylin thought the news of her budding romance with Mr. Kertzner might cheer Aunt Tish up and make her see that love was still alive in the world.

Marylin found Aunt Tish eating a Snickers bar and reading *Scientific American* on the living room couch when she got home from school. Aunt Tish, who was an astronomer, had taken to resting in the afternoon and staying up half the night in the backyard looking at the stars through her telescope. In times of turmoil, she was fond of saying, infinity can be a very comforting concept.

Marylin kept meaning to write that down in her diary.

"He sounds like a dream," Aunt Tish said when Marylin described Mr. Kertzner to her: how every Tuesday he wore his Mickey Mouse tie with the stain in the shape of Texas on it, and how his aftershave smelled just like the nutmeg kringles her father made at Christmas.

"I've always had a fondness for older men myself," Aunt Tish said, handing Marylin half of her Snickers bar. "My first big love was Galileo, who was about four hundred years older than I was at the time. But with a mind like that, you can overlook the little things."

"That's exactly how I feel," Marylin said,

nodding, even though she couldn't exactly remember who Galileo was. "Mr. Kertzner knows everything there is to know about the gypsy moth. I find it fascinating."

This was not entirely true. What Marylin found fascinating was the way Mr. Kertzner practically leaped on top of his desk when describing the gypsy moth's destructive eating habits. It was like somebody had suddenly set his socks on fire.

"Well, maybe we should invite this Mr. Kertzner over to dinner one night," Aunt Tish said. "You could show him the telescope. Fascinating men are always fascinated by telescopes."

It had not occurred to Marylin that you could invite a teacher to your house. When she ran the idea past Flannery the next morning on the bus, Flannery's mouth widened into a humongous O, as though a doctor had just asked to look at her tonsils.

"You can't ask a teacher over to dinner!" Flannery exclaimed. "It just makes the teacher think you're trying to get a better grade from them. Nobody asks teachers to dinner!"

"Why not?" Kate asked from the seat behind Marylin and Flannery. Flannery and Marylin were now speaking to Kate. But Flannery never scooted over to let Kate sit with them, so every morning Kate had to lean forward and rest her chin on the back of their seat if she wanted to join in the conversation. "I bet Mr. Kertzner would like to have dinner at your house."

"Do you really think so?" Marylin asked, craning her neck so she could look at Kate. She ignored Flannery's glare. Flannery didn't like it when Marylin got second opinions.

"Sure," Kate answered. "Just because he's a teacher doesn't mean he's not a human being. Everyone likes being asked over for dinner."

By the time the bus pulled up in front of school, Marylin had made up her mind. She would do it. She would get Aunt Tish to make her famous vegetarian lasagna. She would show Mr. Kertzner Venus through the telescope. At night Venus is called the evening star, Marylin would tell Mr. Kertzner. Next to the sun and the moon, it is the brightest object in the sky.

How could he help but fall in love with her?

"Marylin, can you tell me the stages of the gypsy moth's life span?"

Mr. Kertzner's voice startled Marylin from the daydream she was having about their wedding. In her dream Mr. Kertzner was wearing an emerald-green tuxedo that matched his eyes.

"Um, well," she stammered, trying to shift gears in her brain. "Let's see, there's the pupil stage . . ."

"Yeah, when the gypsy moth starts kindergarten," Matthew Sholls yelled out. Everyone laughed like they thought this was very funny, but Marylin didn't find it funny at all.

"I bet you mean the pupa, don't you?" Mr. Kertzner asked kindly.

Marylin nodded miserably. She wished she were *in* a pupa. She turned around to get a sympathetic look from Ashley Greer, but Ashley was busy rolling her eyes at Elyse Cassill. That's all Marylin needed, to have someone like Ashley Greer turn against her. She'd probably get Flannery turned against her, too, and then Marylin's only friends would be Kate and the wildly destructive gypsy moth.

Mr. Kertzner stopped Marylin on her way out of the classroom for morning break. "Your mom called me last night about having dinner at your house next Tuesday," he told her. "I'm really looking forward to it."

"Really?" Marylin asked. She had thought Mr. Kertzner probably wouldn't want to have anything to do with her after the moth fiasco.

"Sure!" Mr. Kertzner said, smiling. "Usually I just eat TV dinners and watch the news. A home-cooked meal is like a vacation in paradise for me."

Marylin walked out into the hallway feeling as light as a balloon. She decided to learn everything she could about the stars before Tuesday so she could show Mr. Kertzner through Aunt Tish's telescope. Marylin nudged out of her brain the idea that Mr. Kertzner might be more impressed if she learned everything about the gypsy moth before Tuesday. The gypsy moth destroyed fruit crops and was a menace to society, which didn't make it the subject for romance, in Marylin's opinion. The stars, on the other hand, were as romantic as a valentine.

Flannery and Ashley were hanging upside down on the jungle gym when Marylin reached the playground. Flannery was the only seventh grader who hung out during break at the playground. She claimed that so far she hadn't met another kid her age with an IQ over 90. The fact that Flannery chose to spend break with her made Marylin feel like she was practically a teenager.

"I can't believe it! I just can't believe it," Ashley was saying to Flannery, sounding distressed and patting Flannery's upside-down shoulder with her upside-down hand.

"What's wrong?" Marylin asked as she grabbed on to a pole and lifted herself up onto the bar next to Flannery's knees.

"I was just telling Ashley that my doctor says I have really weak ankles," Flannery said, "which means I can't try out for cheerleading."

"Oh," Marylin said, balancing herself on the bar so she wouldn't flip backward or flop forward. She already knew about Flannery's ankles. Flannery's weak ankles were the reason she said she couldn't do a cartwheel. But what was this business about cheerleading?

"I was a cheerleader last year," Flannery continued, swinging back and forth from her knees like a pendulum. "When I lived in Texas. All the best cheerleaders are from Texas. It's a fact."

Ashley peered suspiciously at Marylin. "You're not trying out for cheerleading, are you?"

"Maybe," Marylin said. "I haven't really thought about it."

Flannery pushed herself off the bar with her hands and landed neatly on her feet. "I'll coach you," she told Marylin. "I know all the tricks."

"What about me?" Ashley asked.

Flannery smiled her sweetest smile. "You don't need any coaching. You'll be a shoo-in." She grabbed Marylin's arm, saying, "Come on. I've got to go to the bathroom, and then I'll start giving you advice."

As they walked toward the building, Flannery glanced back at Ashley, who was still hanging upside down on the jungle gym. "Don't you think she sort of looks like a bat, hanging that way?"

Marylin giggled. She was going to be a cheerleader. That would show old Ashley the Bat.

Kate was against the whole idea.

"You'll become the sort of person who only cares about her hair," Kate warned, standing on one foot in the middle of the kitchen and balancing a stack of her sister's *Seventeen* magazines on top of her head in an effort to improve her posture. "I've seen it happen a million times."

"You're only eleven," Marylin said. "You're too young to have seen anything a million times."

"I'll be twelve in two months," Kate reminded Marylin. "Which means I'm older than you are, and therefore wiser. And I know what being a cheerleader does to people, believe me."

Marylin began crumbling a chocolate-chip cookie into little pieces on the kitchen table. It was true that Kate had some experience with cheerleaders. Kate's sister, Tracie, had enjoyed a brief cheerleading career in seventh grade before she made a D in world history and her parents yanked her off the squad. Still, Tracie and Marylin were two completely different people. Marylin had never gotten a D in anything in her life.

"Besides," Kate added, collecting the magazines, which had spilled off her head onto the floor, "do you really think Mr. Kertzner is the type of person who would marry a cheerleader? He's a man of science and reason, don't forget."

Kate was the second and only other person besides Aunt Tish to whom Marylin had told about her feelings for Mr. Kertzner. For all of Kate's drawbacks, like her refusal to pierce her ears, or the way she was always hanging around with little kids like Courtney, Marylin knew she could trust Kate with a secret.

"You don't know, though," Marylin argued with Kate. "Maybe Mr. Kertzner's favorite sister was a cheerleader. Maybe he's crazy about people who are cheerleaders."

Kate shook her head. "All I'm saying is you're taking a big risk. But," she concluded, popping a cookie into her mouth, "it's your life, so go ahead and ruin it if you want to."

All of a sudden Marylin felt like changing the subject. "Hey, let's go sneak into Tracie's room and check out her clothes," she suggested. Tracie had very grown-up taste in clothes, Marylin thought. Most days she looked at least eighteen. Plus sometimes she dated football players. Although Marylin would never admit it to Kate, Tracie was one of her idols.

Kate stared at her, her mouth falling open. "Are you nuts? For one thing, she'd kill us if she caught us. For another thing, the hairspray and cologne perfumes will automatically suffocate you the minute you walk through the door. And for even another thing, who wants to look at Tracie's clothes? Could you have an even more boring idea?"

"It was just a suggestion," Marylin mumbled. She stood up. "I guess I should go home anyway."

"No offense," Kate called after her. "About Tracie's clothes and everything."

Marylin walked home from Kate's the back way, cutting through Mrs. Larch's backyard and following a leafy path through the woods to her house. Flannery's house was smack in the middle between Kate's and Marylin's, and Marylin wasn't in the mood to run into Flannery that afternoon. She'd probably want to practice cheerleading, and right now Marylin's heart just wasn't in it.

It wasn't that Marylin agreed with Kate that she had to choose between cheerleading and

Mr. Kertzner. By the time Marylin was old enough to marry Mr. Kertzner, her cheerleading days would be a thing of the past. By then she'd probably be a world-famous expert on the gypsy moth and Mr. Kertzner would be too stunned by the shining constellation of Marylin's brilliance to care whether or not she'd ever pushed a pom-pom.

But Marylin knew that if she tried out for middle school cheerleading and made it, she might have to choose between Kate and Flannery. Sometimes Marylin felt like a rope being pulled in a tug of war. She didn't know how to get out of the middle, or how to change things.

Marylin didn't even know if she wanted to change things. She was very particular about her life. She liked to know how things were going to be from one day to the next. That's why it drove her crazy when her mother told her in the morning she would make meat loaf for dinner and then her dad decided at five thirty to make spaghetti. It changed the whole tone of Marylin's day.

Aunt Tish was standing at the kitchen sink and peeling potatoes for potato salad when Marylin got home. Marylin hopped up onto the counter next to her to watch.

"You were a cheerleader once, right?" she asked Aunt Tish. Marylin had decided she needed to get the real scoop on cheerleading before she committed herself to something that might completely upset her lifestyle and cause her to care too much about her hair.

Aunt Tish raised her arms into a V and jumped high in the air, yelling, "Rah! Go! Cougars!"

Then she resumed her potato peeling.

"Is that a yes?" Marylin asked.

"T. R. Little High School, the junior varsity squad," Aunt Tish confirmed, nodding. "I did a mean handstand."

Marylin leaned over and pulled a potato peel from Aunt Tish's hair. "Did it change your life? Cheerleading, I mean?"

Aunt Tish thought for a moment. "A little, I guess. It made me more popular and gave me the opportunity to hang out with some pretty snooty girls. But you know what really changed my life?" Aunt Tish's voice grew light and airy, as though she were describing a dream. "The men on the moon."

"You mean the man in the moon, don't you?" Marylin wondered if the potatoes were leaking fumes that were going to Aunt Tish's head.

Aunt Tish laughed. "No, I really mean the men on the moon. I was supposed to go to this horseback-riding camp right before I started tenth grade, but then the astronauts walked on the moon and I was hooked! I watched everything on TV, and instead of begging for a saddle, I begged for a telescope.

"Did you want to become an astronaut too?"

Marylin tried to imagine Aunt Tish in one of those big white astronaut suits, but it was hard to picture. Aunt Tish was more the tailored jacket and jeans type.

"For a little while I did," Aunt Tish said as she started cutting the potatoes into cubes. "But then I realized I didn't really want to walk on the moon; I just wanted to look at it. It captivated me."

"What's captivating about the moon?" Marylin asked, hopping off the counter. This conversation was not teaching her much about cheerleading, she had decided.

Aunt Tish put down her paring knife. "The moon is captivating because it is always changing, but it's always there." She smiled. "Unlike your uncle Nick, who was just always changing."

"Here," Kate said on the bus the next morning, dropping a book onto Marylin's lap before she took her usual seat behind Marylin and Flannery. It was a copy of *A Tale of Two Cities*.

"What are you giving me this for?" Marylin asked.

"Because it's more important to care about your brain than to care about your hair," Kate said. "That's my new motto."

Flannery rolled her eyes. "She is so weird," she said to Marylin in a loud whisper. "I really think we should just ignore her."

Marylin reached down and stuck the book in her backpack next to her nature studies binder and her math homework. "Why should we ignore her?" she whispered back without looking at Flannery. "It's no big deal."

"I can hear every word you're saying," Kate said from behind them.

"That's why we should ignore her," Flannery said.

Marylin really didn't think ignoring Kate was necessary, but you had to be careful about rejecting Flannery's ideas. "I'll think about it, okay?" she said, smiling her most diplomatic smile.

Flannery turned away so that she was facing the aisle. "You can do whatever you want," she said. "I couldn't care less."

It was going to be one of those days, Marylin could tell already.

She was sure of it when Mr. Kertzner assigned Marylin and Jason Frey to be partners for their gypsy moth project. Jason Frey was a toothpick of a boy who barely spoke above a raspy whisper when he was called on in class. Also he always had thin crescents of dirt beneath his fingernails. Marylin was very picky about fingernails. She thought they said a lot about a person.

Marylin scooted her desk next to Jason's. "I guess we should start brainstorming for project ideas," she told him, taking charge. The one nice thing about doing projects with people like Jason Frey was that Marylin got to boss someone else around for a change.

Jason nodded, red splotches blooming along his neck. He looked like he was coming down with an emergency case of the measles.

Suddenly Marylin's left ear was attacked by a wadded-up piece of notebook paper. She looked around as she unfolded it, but no one looked back at her.

Dear Marylin, the note read. *I think you and Jason make a very cute couple. How long have you two been an item? Signed, A Curious Person.*

The writing looked suspiciously like Ashley Greer's when she wrote with her left hand instead of her right.

"How about we brainstorm in silence for a few minutes," Marylin said to Jason, taking a piece of paper out of her nature studies binder.

Jason nodded again. He looked relieved, as though brainstorming out loud with Marylin might have caused him to internally combust right there in the middle of the classroom.

Marylin picked up her pen and began to write. *Dear Ashley,* her note began, *Good luck with cheerleading tryouts! I really mean it a lot!*

Marylin underlined "really" four times. It was clear she needed to do something to get on Ashley's good side, or else Ashley would probably start spreading rumors that Marylin and Jason were planning to elope to Tijuana after social studies.

"Meet me at my house after school," Flannery said as she brushed past Marylin on her way to the playground at morning break. "And whatever you do, don't bring Kate."

"Okay," Marylin said, smiling her biggest, cheeriest smile, the one that showed all her teeth.

"You look like a weasel, smiling that way," Kate said, walking past Marylin on her way to the library.

Marylin leaned her head against the cool,

gray row of lockers outside Mr. Kertzner's classroom. No matter what she did, she just couldn't win with these people.

Mr. Kertzner walked out into the hallway. "Are you feeling sick, Marylin?" he asked, sounding concerned. "Is there anything I can do to help?"

"You could take me to Paris," Marylin said, her head still resting against the lockers.

Mr. Kertzner laughed. "Wouldn't that be a great field trip?

Field trip, shmield trip. Marylin was talking honeymoon.

But all she said was, "Yes, it really would. I think it would be particularly nice to be around all those people who don't speak English."

That way, Marylin thought, she could ignore all of them.

"I'm sorry, honey, but Flannery went to Ashley's house," Flannery's mom told Marylin that afternoon. "Ashley's mom just picked her up about three minutes ago."

"Oh, right, she mentioned that to me on the bus," Marylin lied. "I guess I just forgot."

"I'll tell her you stopped by, sweetie," Flannery's mom said, smiling her nice-mom smile.

Walking back home, Marylin wondered how someone like Flannery ended up with such a pleasant mother. It didn't make any sense. Marylin was beginning to think that the world just didn't add up when you looked at the big picture.

"You look like you need some chocolate," Aunt Tish said when Marylin walked into the kitchen and slumped in a chair.

"It smells too much like onions in here to eat chocolate," Marylin said. "Onions and chocolate don't mix."

"Well, I hope it smells good," Aunt Tish said, stirring a big pot on the stove. "Because this is the tomato sauce for my famous lasagna. Tonight's the big night, after all. Are you excited about Mr. Kertzner coming over?"

Marylin shrugged. She had been more excited a few days ago, when her life had had a nice, even flow to it.

"You know, Aunt Tish," Marylin said, staring up at the ceiling, "sometimes everything in my life is just impossible."

Aunt Tish nodded. "I know exactly what you mean."

At least one thing never changed, Marylin thought. You could always count on Aunt Tish to know exactly what you meant.

And then a horrifying thought occurred to her. Mr. Kertzner was coming over tonight, and she had forgotten to learn everything there was to know about the stars.

"What am I going to do?" Marylin asked Aunt Tish, her voice escalating into a wail.

Aunt Tish turned down the heat on the stove.

"Come on," she said, taking Marylin by the hand. "Some things are less impossible than others."

A handful of stars was pinned against the evening sky when Marylin, Aunt Tish, and Mr. Kertzner walked out to the backyard. Petey followed behind them, humming his favorite songs from *The Lion King*. Petey's humming always drove Marylin crazy, but tonight she was trying to make a good impression on Mr. Kertzner, so she didn't yell at Petey to shut up the way she normally would.

"That was terrific lasagna," Mr. Kertzner said for about the fortieth time. "You're really a great cook, Tish."

"Marylin helped," Aunt Tish told him. "I couldn't have done it without her."

Marylin had thrown the mozzarella cheese on top right before Aunt Tish put the lasagna in the oven. She didn't think she should take credit for the lasagna's overall success. Still, if terrific lasagna was the key to Mr. Kertzner's heart, who was Marylin to inform him she had played a less than major role in this particular lasagna's creation?

The telescope stood in the middle of the backyard, its eye aimed at the Sussmans' house next door.

"Petey's been playing with the telescope again," Marylin said. Ever since Aunt Tish had set up her telescope, Petey had been practically glued to it. Some days he played astronomer, other days he played FBI agent.

"I think Farley Sussman is plotting to overthrow the government," Petey said. Farley, another third grader, was Petey's arch-enemy.

"Farley Sussman couldn't overthrow a hot dog stand," Marylin said.

Aunt Tish and Mr. Kertzner laughed. All night Marylin had noticed that they laughed at exactly the same things. Also, they finished each other's sentences a lot. Marylin was glad they got along so well; it would make things go more smoothly when Marylin and Mr. Kertzner got married. Maybe Aunt Tish could be Marylin's maid of honor.

"Okay, so who's going to show me how to use this thing?" Mr. Kertzner said, nodding toward the telescope. "I'm ready to do some stargazing."

Marylin barely beat Petey to the middle of the backyard. She put her eye to the telescope's viewfinder and searched out the Big Dipper among the crowd of stars that had begun to blossom in the darkening sky. Think soup ladle, Aunt Tish had told her.

"Come look," Marylin called to Mr. Kertzner. "Here's the Big Dipper, which is a part of Ursa Major."

"I had no idea you knew so much about the stars," Mr. Kertzner said, leaning down so he could peer through the telescope.

"Oh, sure," Marylin said casually. "As a matter of fact, the Big Dipper is one of my favorite constellations, along with Cassiopeia, Centaurus, Perseus, and Ursa Minor. I really like all of those a lot."

"I'm impressed," Mr. Kertzner said. "You have the makings of an astronomer."

Marylin beamed. Aunt Tish's advice had worked. Memorize five constellations, Aunt Tish had told her. Most people know only one or two. If you can name five, everyone will think you're an expert.

"Oh, Marylin, look at that moon," Aunt Tish said. "Isn't it beautiful? I love a full moon, even if it is supposed to make people do crazy things."

"What crazy things have you done?" Petey asked Aunt Tish. He sounded as though he were hoping for some helpful hints.

Aunt Tish laughed. "Lots of stuff. Dyed my hair red. Fell in love."

That made Mr. Kertzner laugh too, and his laughter mingled with Aunt Tish's in the cool air and made a kind of song. That was when Marylin saw it, the light of the moon falling over her aunt and her teacher and pulling them together into their own constellation.

Marylin walked over to the telescope and looked through it to the sky filled with stars, so many stars you could never count them all, according to Aunt Tish. If Aunt Tish married Mr. Kertzner, then Mr. Kertzner would be Marylin's uncle, Marylin suddenly realized. If he were her uncle, maybe he wouldn't make Marylin do her gypsy moth project with Jason Frey. Of course, if Mr. Kertzner became her uncle, then Marylin couldn't marry him. She would have to find someone else to fall in love with.

Marylin pointed the telescope toward the moon. It was perfectly round, without any ragged edges or weird bumps. Most things in life were full of ragged edges and weird bumps, Marylin thought, no matter how perfect they looked from a distance. Even love. Even your best friends.

"You know, I was thinking about trying out for cheerleading," Marylin said, as much to the moon as to anyone else. She combed her fingers through her hair. She would have to be careful not to care about her hair too much, or else Kate would never let her hear the end of it.

"That's great!" Aunt Tish exclaimed. "I'll come to your tryouts. I know you'll make it."

"I was a cheerleader in college," Mr. Kertzner said. "It's a lot of fun."

Petey started laughing. "Boys can't be cheerleaders!" he yelled.

Mr. Kertzner picked Petey up and held him upside down. "Boys can be anything they want!"

"Me too," Marylin said to the moon. "What do you think about that?"

The moon didn't answer. It just kept on its slow orbit around the earth, the way it had for millions of years. It would always be there, Marylin knew, watching over her, covering her with its shimmering light.

the magic kingdom

To be honest, Kate wasn't all that sorry her parents had unplugged the TV. She was getting tired of seeing all those perfect people parading across the screen every night. It was the perfect kids who bugged her the most—those gaggles of sisters with moonbeam-blond hair that bounced and flounced all over the place. A person with bone-straight, plain-brown hair really had no business tuning in.

For a person with bone-straight, plain-brown hair and a stomach that looked a little bit like she'd stuck an upside-down cereal bowl beneath her shirt, TV was not a good idea at all. None of the moonbeam-blond sisters ever had cereal-bowl stomachs. The sisters under twelve were as skinny as lizards, and the sisters over twelve had mountain-range curves that made all the boys on the shows go bug-eyed and yell, "Whoa!"

On the whole, Kate preferred books.

"Are you at least allowed to watch videos?" Marcie Grossman asked at lunch on Tuesday when Kate had announced her parents' no-more-TV rule. Marcie's voice trembled a bit, as though Kate's parents were ax murderers who might come after her next.

"Sometimes on weekends we can," Kate said. "But only ones my parents approve of."

"No one's going to want to come over to your house anymore, that's for sure," Marcie said, biting into her tomato sandwich.

"Life does not revolve around TV," Kate said, repeating her parents' latest motto. "Anyway, who cares?"

"I'd come over to your house," Paisley Clark offered matter-of-factly from where she sat by herself at the far end of the cafeteria table. "My mother doesn't let me watch TV either. Not even videos on weekends."

A single, skinny bean sprout danced at the corner of Paisley's mouth as she spoke. In the three weeks that Paisley had been at their school, Kate had noticed she was the sort of person who often had things stuck to her. Once she came to school with three raisins stuck to the back of her sweater; another time she had a stamp stuck to her elbow. But Paisley never seemed embarrassed when these things were pointed out to her. She just laughed. Sometimes she didn't even bother unsticking what was stuck.

"I guess you probably read a lot," Kate said as off-handedly as she could. It was a simple statement, but beneath it ran the dot and dash of a secret code.

"All the time," Paisley answered. She held up a copy of *Number the Stars*. "Even at lunch."

Kate and Paisley looked at each other for several seconds, then nodded almost imperceptibly, as though something had been agreed upon between them. Which was why Kate was not the least bit surprised when Paisley saved her a seat on the bus that afternoon, even though Paisley did not normally ride Kate's bus home.

"I'll call my mom when we get to your house," Paisley said. "She can pick me up after work. Did you ever read *Tuck Everlasting*?"

Kate slid down in the seat and propped her knees against the seat in front of her. "Read it?" she asked Paisley, raising her eyebrows as high as they would go. "I've practically memorized it."

At the very beginning of spring, weeks before anyone even knew Paisley Clark existed, everything about sixth grade changed. It was as if a mysterious force had taken over. The sixth grade had gotten shuffled like a deck of cards and been dealt into entirely new groups. At lunchtime kids walked to their tables as though an invisible hand were guiding them to where they were supposed to be. The weird thing to Kate was that no one ever tried to switch tables or join a new group. Everyone just seemed to accept the decisions the mysterious force had made.

The mysterious force had thrown Kate in with Marcie Grossman, Amber Colbaugh, and Timma Phipps. There was a certain logic to it, Kate had to admit. They certainly were not a group of perfect TV people. Marcie had blond, bouncy hair, but usually it bounced in the wrong direction. None of them ever said snazzy, smart-alecky things to Mrs. Watson in class. Boys teased them, but not the cute boys, and not in a way that made their hearts open up like windows in springtime.

Every day at lunch Kate, Marcie, Amber, and Timma gathered at the last table in the second row by the "Olympic Dreams of the Sports Superstars" mural and unwrapped their sandwiches. From where she sat, Kate had a perfect view of the second table in the first row by the emergency exit door. That was where Marylin sat with Mazie Calloway and the other middle school cheerleaders. That was where Marylin sat acting like Kate was some person she might have known a long time ago but whose name she couldn't quite remember.

"So what was it like to spend the night at Marylin's?" Amber or Timma might ask, gazing at Marylin and the cheerleaders. They asked these questions as if Marylin were a movie star. "What's her room like?" Marcie might ask. "Is her mom nice?"

Sometimes Kate answered their questions with a bored sort of authority. "Up until third grade Marylin wore footie pajamas," Kate would tell them, practically yawning, as if to say, *So what? Who cares? It's just Marylin. No big deal.*

Other times Kate leaned back in her chair, her arms folded over her chest, her mouth set into a scowl, and said, "You know, just because someone is popular doesn't mean they're a great person or anything. Just because someone's popular doesn't mean everything about them is interesting."

On those occasions Marcie, Timma, and Amber just stared at her. Marcie in particular looked like she thought maybe she should take Kate's temperature.

Paisley hadn't watched TV in five years. She had been too busy backpacking all over the world with her mother, whom Paisley referred to as Phoebe.

"Phoebe really liked Tunisia, but I liked Italy

the best," Paisley told Kate one afternoon as they sat under the beech tree by the kickball field and braided friendship bracelets for each other. "I know that's what everyone says and it's a totally boring choice, but I can't help it. Italy is where the best food is. Much better than in New Zealand or Pakistan."

Kate nodded, as though she had some idea of what the food tasted like in New Zealand or Pakistan.

"I liked the bread in Germany, but once I got really sick on a piece of wienerschnitzel I ate in Freiberg," Paisley continued. "I mean, I threw up all over this lady on the train. So Germany is definitely not on my top-ten-best-food-countries list."

Paisley, it turned out, had lists for everything. She had a list of all the books she had read, and one of her favorite restaurants, and one of the birds she had spotted while hiking in the Pyrenees. She even had a list of all the boys she had kissed. So far there was only one name on that list: James. Paisley had met James at a travelers' hostel in England. All she really remembered about him was that he had been very polite.

"He kissed me and then he shook my hand," Paisley said as she handed Kate her finished friendship bracelet. "It was a very English thing for him to do."

Kate examined the bracelet's blue-and-green weave and then held out her arm so Paisley could tie the bracelet around her wrist. She felt like a princess receiving a present from a good fairy. Kate was beginning to think there was something magic about Paisley. For one thing, the mysterious force seemed to have no effect on her whatsoever. In fact, when Paisley was around, the mysterious force seemed to loosen its grip on everyone.

Kate had first noticed this the week before when, in front of everyone, Andrew O'Shea had walked over to their table right before the end of lunch. Andrew usually sat with Trevor Parlier and Jason Frey. They were the sort of boys who were always dropping their lunch trays by accident and tripping over cracks in the sidewalk. Trevor Parlier had something wrong with his feet and had to wear special shoes, and Jason's sweaters always smelled kind of funny, like maybe he let his dog sleep on them.

"Hey, Paisley," Andrew said brightly, adjusting his glasses, "you think you could look over my social studies paper on Greece for me? I figured since you've been there and everything, you might be able to tell me if my report is any good or not."

"Sure," Paisley answered with a smile. "Bring it on over."

Kate looked around the table to see if Marcie, Amber, and Timma were making gagging faces or rolling their eyes. But no one seemed the least bit concerned, even when Trevor and Jason followed Andrew back to their table. They all actually laughed when Trevor said, "I tried reading Andrew's paper, but it was Greek to me."

"I read this book last summer about this girl who lived in ancient Greece," Paisley said as she took Andrew's paper from him. "It was really cool. See, her parents were slaves. . . ."

Everyone leaned toward Paisley as she told the story. Jason Frey reached over and gently plucked a piece of lettuce off of her collar. Amber smiled at Trevor.

There was no doubt about it. Paisley was magic.

Kate's parents had unplugged the TV after they caught Tracie watching an R-rated movie on a cable channel. Mr. and Mrs. Faber were against young girls watching R-rated movies.

There will be time enough for that later, they told their daughters. There will be plenty of time when you girls are grown up to fill your brains with junk.

Paisley's mom had a bumper sticker on her VW bug that read KILL YOUR TELEVISION. Kate saw it the day Phoebe came to pick up Paisley after lunch to take her to the orthodontist. Paisley was going to get braces.

"Purple ones," Paisley had told Kate on the phone the night before. "I'll be the only kid I know with purple teeth."

After Kate got off the phone, she picked up her copy of *Bridge to Terabithia* and plopped down on the couch in the living room. The TV stared blankly at her from the corner. That was another thing about TV, Kate thought. It never had any kids on it with purple braces. All the moonbeam-blond sisters had perfect teeth. So did Kate, for that matter, but just then she wished her bicuspids had been a little bit crooked. Kate would choose blue braces, to go with her eyes.

"Hey, it's Purple Paisley!"

Robbie Ballard leaned over from his desk at the beginning of social studies and made a face in Paisley's direction. Robbie Ballard was one of the cute boys who said nice things only to the middle school cheerleaders.

"I know," Paisley said laughing, her purple braces flashing beneath the classroom's fluorescent lights. "Phoebe says I look like a petunia."

"Phoebe? Phoebe?" Robbie Ballard squawked. He poked Wes Porter in the side. "Phoebe says Purple Paisley looks like a petunia!"

"Yuck! Yuck!" Wes Porter croaked back. Behind him, Mazie Calloway and Marylin giggled.

Paisley shrugged, still smiling. "Phoebe likes flowers," she said. She didn't sound the least bit offended.

It was Paisley's turn to give her social studies report to the class. Instead of having her do a regular report on just one country, Mrs. Watson had asked Paisley to discuss all the different places she and Phoebe had traveled. Paisley lugged a large shopping bag to the front of the room. The first thing she pulled out of the bag was a long strand of beads.

"Phoebe and I got these in Kenya, in a place called Samburu," Paisley began, handing the beads to Matthew Sholls in the first row. "The day we got them, this little brown dog tried to adopt us. See, we were hiking through this village . . ."

Everyone in the class sat mesmerized as Paisley continued to talk and pass around the things she pulled from her shopping bag. Here was a red-and-yellow serape someone had given Phoebe in Ecuador. Next came a turban like the kind bedouin men wore in Egypt.

Everyone laughed and clapped when Matthew Sholls tried on the kilt Paisley had picked up in Yemen; it was called a futa, and men wore them all the time there.

"That was fun," Paisley told Kate after social studies, when they were sitting at their usual cafeteria table by the "Olympic Dreams of the Sports Superstars" mural. "I'd forgotten I had half that stuff. Phoebe and I were up practically all night digging through storage boxes."

"I really liked your report," Andrew O'Shea said, sitting down next to Paisley. "One day I'm going to go to all those places too."

"Weren't you afraid of catching some terrible disease?" Marcie wanted to know. Marcie was the sort of person who worried a lot about catching terrible diseases.

"I heard camels are really stubborn," Jason Frey said, scooting a chair in between Amber and Timma. "Is that true?"

"Did you ever ride in a caravan?" Trevor

Parlier asked as he dropped his lunch bag down next to Kate's.

"Great braces, Paisley."

Everyone looked up. Mazie Calloway was standing in the aisle next to Paisley's chair.

"Why don't you come over and sit with us?" Mazie asked Paisley, nodding toward the middle school cheerleaders' table. "Ashley wants to check out your braces. She might get some just like them."

Paisley smiled her purple smile. "Why don't you come sit over here?" she asked Mazie. "We can make room for everyone."

I will remember this day for the rest of my life, Kate thought as she watched a gaggle of moonbeam-blond middle school cheerleaders with lizard-skinny legs troop with their lunch trays toward Kate's table.

"There's room for everyone," Paisley said as she pulled more chairs to the table. "Plenty of room."

·····

Later Kate wished Paisley's social studies report hadn't been such a big hit. Maybe if Paisley had just handed around postcards from her travels, Mrs. Watson and Ms. Carter-Juarez, the school principal, would not have decided Paisley should be in a magnet school for Accelerated Children.

"Accelerated Children? What does that mean?" Kate asked the night Paisley called to tell her about the new school. "Do you have motors stuck on you to make you go faster?"

"I think it just means they let you work at your own pace," Paisley explained. "I hope the kids there think purple braces are okay."

Kate knew that wherever Paisley went, the kids would think her purple braces were okay. Paisley had that effect on people. She made you forget about stupid stuff like cheerleading and who was supposed to sit at what table. Hanging out with Paisley the last few weeks,

Kate had realized how much stuff like cheer-leading and talking about kissing boys bored her. It occurred to her that maybe she was the one who was leaving Marylin behind, when she'd always thought before that Marylin was the one who had left. It made her feel a little guilty, to be honest. Poor Marylin, fated to live such an automatically boring life while Kate got to do all kinds of interesting stuff with Paisley.

The next day at lunch the cafeteria felt like Paisley had never been there. The middle school cheerleaders sat at their table in the first row by the emergency exit door and pre-tended that no one else existed. Kate saw Andrew O'Shea trip over thin air and nearly drop his lunch tray on the way to his old seat by Trevor Parlier and Jason Frey. It seemed that as soon as the mysterious force had found out Paisley was at a different school, it had taken over again.

"I heard that Mazie's dad owns the Fairview Country Club," Amber said chewing on a carrot. "He's not just a member; he owns it."

"I wonder what her house is like," Marcie said. "Do you think her mom is nice?"

Kate picked at her turkey sandwich. It looked flat, as though the mysterious force had gotten into her bag and squashed her lunch.

I've had just about enough of this, she thought.

Kate carefully wrapped up her squashed turkey sandwich and put it back in her lunch bag. Then she stood up.

"Where are you going?" Marcie asked. "Are you sick?"

Kate marched resolutely to Andrew O'Shea's table. "Scoot over," she told Trevor as she pulled up a chair. "Anyone want to trade for a turkey sandwich?"

Then she turned and looked toward her old table by the "Olympic Dreams of the Sports Superstars" mural. Marcie, Amber, and Timma were staring at her, their faces full of wonder.

"Well?" Kate called to them, raising her eyebrows as high as they would go. "What are you waiting for?"

kiss

There weren't any bleachers at the soccer field, so all the parents who came to watch the game had to bring their own chairs or else stand up. Marylin's mom was sitting on a long, folded-out beach chair next to the drama club's bake sale table. She was dressed in a business suit and had a laptop computer on her knees. Marylin wished her mom had dressed in sweats and tennis shoes like all the other mothers. It was hard for her to concentrate on cheerleading with her mom sticking out like a sore thumb.

"Go, Mavericks!" Ashley Greer yelled, and then all the cheerleaders were yelling, "We're number one!" and "We're the best!" Marylin yelled out, "Go, team!" as loud as she could and jumped up and down.

"Go, Wes!" a voice called from behind her. Marylin turned around to see a boy leaning against a bike, one fist raised in the air. He had dark-brown hair, and eyes that were so blue, Marylin could see that they were blue from ten feet away.

"That's Wes Porter's brother," Mazie Calloway said in a loud whisper to Marylin. "He's only got one leg."

"I see two legs," Marylin said. "How could he ride a bike with only one leg?"

Mazie shook her head, as though she couldn't believe how dumb Marylin was. "One of his legs is fake. He had cancer last year, when he was in, like, seventh grade."

The boy didn't look like the sort of person

who'd had cancer to Marylin. He looked like her cousin Shelton, who was always building forts in his backyard and then tearing them down. You had to be pretty healthy to destroy things the way her cousin Shelton did.

"Are you sure he had cancer?" she asked Mazie.

Mazie nodded. "Positive."

"Team Appreciation Cheer!" Jessica Donovan called out. Jessica was an eighth grader who was the captain of the cheerleaders. Marylin got in line with the other girls and faced the crowd. She put on her best cheerleader smile. She tried not to notice that Wes Porter's brother was smiling back at her. Too much interpersonal contact with team supporters was not professional, according to Ms. Lyttle, the cheerleading coach.

During half-time Marylin's mom brought her a juice box. "You're working hard out here," she said. "You need your vitamins."

"Hey, Mrs. McIntosh," Mazie said. "So how do we look? Better than the team, that's for sure."

The team was behind four to nothing. Marylin hoped it wasn't the cheerleaders' fault. During the first half they had accidentally done a basketball cheer during an important penalty shot. Wes Porter's brother had yelled out, "Hey, wrong sport!" and a bunch of people in the crowd had laughed.

"You all look wonderful," Marylin's mom assured Mazie. "Maybe the team will have a better second half."

"Excuse me, ma'am?" Wes Porter's brother stood behind Marylin's mom. He was holding a dirt-crusted glove. "Did you drop this?"

Marylin's mom peered at the glove. "No, that looks like it's been out here awhile. But it's nice of you to ask," she said, smiling at the boy.

"Okay," the boy said, sounding disappointed. He looked at Marylin. "You didn't drop this glove, did you?" he asked. Marylin shook her head no.

The boy shrugged. "Oh, well," he said, and then he let the glove fall to the ground. Marylin watched as he walked back over to his bike. You would never know he had only one leg, Marylin thought. He walked exactly like a two-legged person.

The team lost five to one. By the end of the game the cheerleaders' jumps barely lifted them off the ground. Marylin's voice sounded like someone had rubbed sandpaper over the top of it. She sort of liked it that way, though. It made her sound older.

"My mom will take us to the party tonight," Caitlin Moore told Marylin as they were packing up their cheerleading gear. "Be ready at seven thirty, okay?"

Marylin nodded. She waved at the other cheerleaders as they walked off toward the parking lot. Marylin's mom was standing on the field talking to the school principal, Ms. Carter-Juarez. Looking around to make sure no one was paying attention, Marylin picked up the glove that Wes Porter's brother had let drop to the ground and stuffed it into her coat pocket.

I think I have one just like it at home, she had been prepared to say if anyone caught her. But no one did, so she didn't have to make up an excuse for taking something just because Wes Porter's brother had touched it.

"So who's going to be at this party?" Marylin's mom asked that night ten minutes before Marylin was supposed to leave. "Anybody I should know about? Any cute boys?"

"Mom!" Marylin pretended she was shocked her mother would ask such a thing.

Marylin's mom plopped down on the edge of Marylin's bed. "What? Can't I be curious about the cute boys in your class?"

Petey came to the doorway. "You're too old for cute boys, Mom," he said. "You have to stick to Dad."

"Thanks a lot!" Marylin's mom said, throwing a pillow at Petey. "Just my luck."

Marylin ignored her mom's last remark. In her opinion, if her mom could find a few nicer things to say about her dad, maybe they wouldn't fight so much and her dad wouldn't always been gone on business trips. Maybe Marylin could grow up in a happy home.

But she kept her opinion to herself, since she wasn't in the mood to discuss her parents' relationship. Instead she looked in the mirror for the ten millionth time. She thought her hair might look really stupid. All the other cheerleaders had great hair. They had award-winning hair. Marylin's hair was just okay, as far as she was concerned. For a minute she considered dying it, and then she remembered what she'd been meaning to tell her mom ever since she got home from the game.

"Flannery cut off all of her hair and dyed it red!" Marylin exclaimed. "She looks like she just got back from outer space. She's so weird now!"

"You're kidding," Marylin's mom said. "I can't believe Penny would let her do something like that."

"I don't think she asked her mom if she could. I think she just went ahead and did it."

Marilyn pulled at her bangs, wondering if braids would look good. Braids were out of the question for Flannery now, that was for sure. She barely had enough hair to run a comb through. She wondered if Flannery missed wearing braids. That's what she had worn for the cheerleading tryouts.

"I guess I'll try out after all," Flannery had told Marylin, way back when practically the entire middle school had been buzzing about who had a chance to make the cheerleading squad and who didn't. Only people like Kate acted like they didn't care.

"What about your ankles?" Marylin had asked. "Didn't your doctor say you couldn't try out because of your ankles?"

Flannery shrugged. "He said they were better. He was more worried what it would do to a natural cheerleader like me not to be on the squad. Really, it's like breathing. Someone like me needs to cheer to survive. I realized that after coaching you all that time. I only hope I don't bump you off the squad."

When Marylin walked into the gym for tryouts, she saw the members of last year's cheerleading squad congregated by a table at the far end of the basketball court. Marylin noted that they all had long necks, like swans in warm-up clothes. They chatted amiably among themselves and raised knowing eyebrows at one another as they surveyed the nervous group of girls flittering around the edges of the gym, chirping like nervous sparrows.

Finally the tallest cheerleader stood up and blew a whistle. Everyone quieted. "When I call out your name, please come front and center and show us your routine. Remember, be loud, be proud, and smile!"

The cheerleaders behind her whooped and applauded, and a few of the girls in the crowd did too. Marylin thought maybe she should jump up and down, but she didn't want to draw too much attention to herself, in case the panel of cheerleaders thought she was show-offy. Although, if you thought about it, cheerleaders were sort of supposed to be show-offy. By the time Marylin had decided maybe she'd clap just a little bit, everyone else had stopped, so she just stood there quietly.

The first few girls who tried out were awful. Marylin knew she shouldn't be happy that some people couldn't do a cartwheel to save their lives, but she couldn't help herself. Then

Ashley Greer was called. You could just tell she was a natural cheerleader, the way she bounced on the balls of her feet and smiled so hard it made Marylin's face hurt to look at her. "Ready, okay!" Ashley yelled, and then she went into her routine. The cheerleaders behind the table began scratching rapid notes on their clipboards. Ashley was in, you could just tell.

When Marylin's name was called, she ran to the center of the court, thinking, *Bounce! Bounce! Bounce!* And then, to her horror, she yelled "Bounce!" at the top of her lungs and everyone giggled. "Bounce!" she yelled again, hoping it would seem like she'd done it on purpose the first time.

"Bounce, everyone! Get on your feet!" Marylin bounced a few times herself when she hit front and center, and suddenly it was as if she'd bounced herself into another person. All the jittery nervousness that had filled her like helium a few moments before magically became superpowered cheerleading energy surging through her arms and legs. "Ready, okay!" she shouted, not caring that she was copying Ashley. It just sounded like the professional, cheerleading sort of thing to say.

As she clapped and stomped her way through her routine, Marylin noticed the cheerleaders behind the table scribbling on their clipboards. Her smile brightened by several hundred watts. She was in, she could just feel it.

She was in, that was, if Flannery didn't push her off the squad. Marylin leaned back against the gym wall as Flannery tromped out to the center of the court. Flannery nodded at the panel of judges, then put her hands on her hips. "Let's go!" she called.

But Flannery didn't go. Marylin wasn't an expert or anything, but she'd seen enough cheerleaders in action to know that you had to have a special quality to cheer. You had to look like you were light as air and strong as steel at the same time. You needed to look like a boy could lift your entire body up on his little finger, and as if you could do a triple flip off his fingertips.

Flannery looked like she needed a nap. There was just something about the way she stomped across the floor. It was more like a really old person who was mad about something shuffling down the hallway to tell you about it. She didn't lift her arms up high enough. And halfway through her routine, she started scowling instead of smiling.

"You did great!" Marylin lied when Flannery had finished, and Flannery nodded, a confident grin on her face. "I aced it!" she said. "I'm just a natural, I guess!"

When Flannery got cut after the first round of tryouts, she wasn't exactly gracious about it. "I guess I didn't bribe the right people," she said so that all the cheerleaders at the judges' table could hear her. Marylin found herself slowly edging away from her, so that nobody would put the two of them together in their minds.

The next week Flannery had started hanging out with Bebe Hurst and Trish Simon, two well-known eighth grade cigarette smokers. Marylin had felt sort of bad about it, but she was so busy learning cheers and smiling all the time, well, there hadn't been a whole lot she could do, except give Flannery friendly waves in the hallway. Of course, it was Marylin's job now to give everyone friendly waves in the hallway, but she tried to make her waves to Flannery especially cheerful.

"I guess it's a good thing for Flannery that hair grows out," Marylin's mom said. "So is she going to be at this party tonight?"

Marylin shook her head. "I think it's just going to be sixth grade cheerleaders and soccer players." And maybe Wes Porter's brother, she hoped, since the party was at Wes Porter's house. She'd been thinking about him all afternoon. She kept forgetting he had only one leg.

"When was your first real kiss with Dad?" Marylin asked her mom now, trying to remember exactly what Wes Porter's brother looked like. "Did it just happen, or is it something you planned?"

"What a question!" her mom said, laughing. "I guess it just happened. We were at a costume party. He was dressed up like Elmer Fudd."

"What did your friends think about him?"

Marylin's mom considered this for a second. "I don't remember. I'm sure it didn't matter. When you think you've found the right person, you don't care much what other people think."

Marylin knew she shouldn't care what other people thought, but she did. That was one of the main drawbacks of being a cheerleader. It was practically her job to care what other people thought.

Marylin's mom came over to the mirror and began brushing Marylin's hair. "Do you want me to French braid it?" she asked.

Marylin started to giggle. "French braid" made her think of "French kiss." She wondered exactly what kind of kissing would go on at this party tonight. She'd never been kissed, not romantically anyway. When Marylin daydreamed about kissing, usually it was with Robbie Ballard, although he was a little more mature in her daydreams than he was in real life. Marylin had strong feelings that kissing should be serious. To make her daydreams come out right, she had to put out of her mind how often Robbie Ballard used the word *booger* on a daily basis.

Marylin liked to daydream about kissing in the part of a restaurant you waited in until the waiter came and took you to your table. She also felt kissing on a balcony of a hotel overlooking the beach would be nice. In her dreams she and the mature Robbie looked at each other a long time before they kissed, and then he gently swiped a strand of hair from her eyes before leaning toward her, lips puckered.

Marylin looked at her reflection in the mirror again. If she was going to get kissed in the serious, romantic fashion of her daydreams, she definitely needed to do something about her hair. "A French braid would be great," she told her mother.

"I think you should dye your hair like Flannery did," Petey offered from the doorway. "I think it would be cool to look like something from outer space."

Marylin and her mom groaned in unison. You just couldn't expect some people to understand about hair.

There was a rumor that Wes Porter's parents were going to be out of town that night, which meant there would be no grown-ups at the party.

"His parents better be there!" Caitlin Moore's mother exclaimed one block away from Wes Porter's house. "No daughter of mine is going to an unchaperoned party before she reaches the age of twenty-one!"

Caitlin groaned. "Mom, don't make such a big deal out of everything. No one else's parents care."

Marylin kept quiet. She knew her parents would care whether or not the party was chaperoned. They just hadn't thought to ask.

"I highly doubt that no one else's parents care," Caitlin's mom said as she pulled the car into the Porters' driveway. She opened her door. "I'm going to find out exactly what's going on here."

Marylin and Caitlin stayed as far behind Caitlin's mom as they could. *What a terrible way to come to a party*, Marylin thought.

It didn't matter that she wasn't even related to Caitlin's mom. Everyone would think they were connected.

Mrs. Porter answered the door. She was wearing jeans and a sweatshirt with a picture of a cat in a tuxedo painted on it. "Of course we'll be here for the entire party," she reassured Caitlin's mom. "I bet I know how this misunderstanding got started. Wes's brother, Tyler, is going to stay in the room while the party is going on, while Mike and I stay upstairs. That way there'll be some supervision without actual grown-ups putting a damper on the kids' fun."

Marylin could tell Caitlin's mom thought both Mr. and Mrs. Porter should be hovering over the party every second, but she couldn't actually complain as long as there were parents somewhere in the house.

Robbie Ballard was standing in the kitchen throwing potato chips at Wes when Marylin and Caitlin finally made it inside. "Wow, is your mom overprotective or what?" Robbie said to Caitlin.

"Shut up, Robbie," Caitlin said, but she giggled when she said it.

Wes put his arm around Marylin's shoulder. "Now, Marylin—her mom wouldn't care at all, would she? That's why Marylin's such a cool girl."

Marylin slipped out of her coat and slipped out from under Wes's arm at the same time. "So where's the party?" she asked, handing her coat to Wes. "Are we the first ones here?"

"Basement," Robbie said through a mouthful of potato chips. "We just came up to get some more stuff to eat."

Marylin followed Robbie and Caitlin down the stairs. Wes was right behind her, tugging on her French braid. "Quit!" she told Wes, slapping at his hand. "You're messing up my hair."

"Ooh, touchy, aren't we?" Wes said in a

teasing voice. "We wouldn't want to mess up Marylin's hair, now, would we?"

"Leave her alone, Wes." Wes's brother was sitting in an easy chair in the corner of the basement near the staircase. He held a copy of *Sports Illustrated* opened to a picture of a bunch of football players tangled up in a pile. Marylin wondered if looking at people playing sports made him sad. Although for all she knew he could play whatever sport he wanted to. He could ride a bike, after all.

"Shut up, Ty," Wes told him. He turned to Marylin and Caitlin. "Ignore him. My parents are paying him to stay down here."

Ty smiled at Marylin. "I'll be your baby-sitter for the evening. Your hair looks nice, by the way."

Marylin smiled right back at him. She couldn't help it.

"Marylin! Get over here!" Mazie yelled from

the far side of the room, where she was standing with the other cheerleaders by the refreshments table. There were Ruby and Ashley and Mazie, and now Marylin and Caitlin. They all gave her little sideways hugs when she joined them, squealing, their squeals sounding like tiny little cheers. Marylin had never had the sort of friends who squealed before. Kate could yell with the best of them, but she was definitely not a squealer.

Kate! The bottom of Marylin's stomach felt like it had dropped right out. She'd been supposed to go to Kate's after school on Wednesday! It had even been Marylin's idea, after their cheerleading coach, Ms. Lyttle, had talked to them about being active members of their community. Marylin had promised she would help Kate bake cookies for her church bake sale. That seemed like the sort of thing an active community member did. But then Mazie had asked her to come over Wednesday afternoon to work on cheers, and Marylin had forgotten all about cookie baking. Well, that explained why Kate had hardly said a word to her on the bus.

Marylin sighed. The hard part about having so many new friends was that the old ones got lost in the shuffle. Being a cheerleader was like having a whole flock of best friends, friends who just couldn't seem to stop squealing. In fact Ashley and Caitlin were now squealing for no apparent reason at all. Marylin looked around. The cheerleaders were the only girls there. Counting Wes and Robbie, but not Ty, there were seven boys. All the lamps in the room were covered with scarves, so that only a dim light filled the room. Marylin shivered, even though it wasn't the least bit cold.

"It's so weird that Wes's brother has to

sit down here with us," Ashley said, looking over at Ty.

"He only has one leg," Mazie said, grabbing a cookie from the table. "Did you guys know that?"

Caitlin squealed. "Really? How weird! Why does he only have one leg?"

"Cancer," Mazie told her.

Marylin wished Mazie would quit making such a big deal about Ty's leg. Who cared? Anyone could tell that he was a very nice person, and wasn't that what really mattered? *I should stick up for him*, Marylin thought. But she had no idea what she should say, so she didn't say anything.

Marylin watched as Wes and Ned Garza, another boy from the soccer team, started pounding each other with pillows from the couch. Five seconds later all the boys except for Ty were bashing each other with pillows and couch cushions.

"Is this a party or a wrestling match?" Ruby called out. Ruby was the prettiest cheerleader, in Marylin's opinion, and it fascinated her how boys automatically did whatever they could to make Ruby like them. One by one the boys dropped their pillows and cushions and stood up, their arms hanging awkwardly at their sides, as though they didn't know what to do with themselves if it didn't involve inflicting bodily harm.

Robbie socked Wes in the shoulder. "Let's get this show on the road, bro," he said.

Wes nodded, then looked around as if he were waiting for suggestions. Ned Garza grabbed a bag of chips that had been perched on a rocking chair and began piling one chip after another into his mouth, little potato chip crumbs spilling down the front of his shirt.

"Very charming," Ty said, turning the page of his magazine.

Marylin giggled, and Mazie gave her a funny look. "What are you laughing at?" she asked, and then she nudged Marylin with her shoulder.

"Yeah, Marylin," Caitlin said, laughing and banging into her from the other side. "What are you laughing at?"

"Is it against the law to laugh in here?" Marylin asked, banging back into Caitlin. Suddenly all the girls were knocking into one another and laughing hysterically.

Robbie held up a soda bottle and cleared his throat. The girls went silent. "Okay, ladies and gentlemen! It's time for the games to begin!"

Ruby and Ashley and Mazie giggled some more. They had been waiting all year to play spin the bottle, and finally they were going to get their chance. "Come on!" Ruby said in a loud whisper, bumping into Mazie to get her to walk to the middle of the room, where Robbie stood holding the bottle.

"For crying out loud, Ballard, were you born yesterday?" Ty asked from his chair. "You can't play spin the bottle with an empty plastic bottle! It won't spin on a carpet. Go get a glass Coke bottle from upstairs."

"Does he really have to hang out down here?" Robbie asked Wes.

Wes shrugged his shoulders. "It beats having my mom down here." Then he ran upstairs to get the Coke bottle.

"Round and round and round she goes!" Robbie called out after Wes had handed him the new bottle. He flicked the bottle's neck to start it spinning. The first time it stopped, it pointed at Ned Garza. "I don't think so," Robbie said, spinning the bottle again. This time it pointed at Ashley. "Much better!"

Everyone laughed and cheered when Robbie leaned across the circle to kiss Ashley. It was just a tiny kiss, the sort of kiss Marylin gave her grandparents when they came for a visit.

Is this what everyone gets so excited about? Marylin wondered. Suddenly she felt very disappointed, like the time her aunt Phyllis had given her three blouses and four pairs of underwear for Christmas instead of the Beauty Pageant Barbie she'd been expecting.

Next it was Ashley's turn to spin. She got Walker Marley, whose kiss barely brushed her lips. Then Walker spun the bottle so hard that it careened around the circle, landing on Marylin's foot.

"It's a bottle, not a bottle rocket, Walker," Ty commented, walking over to the refreshment table. "Try not to take anyone's eye out with it, huh?"

It was Marylin's first kiss. When Walker leaned toward her, a buzzing filled her ears. Marylin thought she might faint, but instead of swooning she found herself panicking that her nose would get in the way. What in the world was she supposed to do with her nose?

She twisted her head at the very last second, so that Walker almost missed her lips completely. His upper lip smushed briefly against the corner of her mouth before he pulled his face away.

It wasn't the most romantic kiss a girl could get, and Marylin didn't feel at all different afterward. She'd expected romantic feelings to fill her like music after her first kiss. Instead she found herself wondering what Kate was doing at that very second. Probably something relaxing and fun, like watching TV and eating popcorn.

"All right, Marylin!" Mazie yelled. "Now show those boys how it's done!"

Marylin looked around the circle, wondering whom she should aim for. She really wasn't in the mood to kiss anyone at that very second, but Robbie Ballard might not be so bad. She wouldn't mind it if it got around the sixth grade that she had kissed Robbie Ballard.

She closed her eyes and gave the bottle a twirl. When she opened her eyes, the bottle was pointed at the gap between Wes and Caitlin, its mouth aimed directly at Ty, who was eating potato chips next to the table.

"Oh my God," Caitlin said. "It's pointing at Ty! You have to kiss Ty!" She said this as though it were the worst thing she could imagine having to do.

All the rest of the girls shrieked with laughter. Marylin could tell they all thought kissing Ty was a terrible idea. Maybe she was supposed to think that way too. Maybe she was supposed to think that kissing a boy with only one leg and who used to have cancer was not something a cheerleader did. But at that very minute Marylin didn't care what she was supposed to think.

Ty smiled at her, the same smile he'd been smiling at her all day. "It's not my party, but I can't argue with the bottle," he said, shrugging, as though he had no choice but to kiss Marylin. It didn't look like he felt too bad about it, Marylin thought. She smiled back at him as he moved into the circle.

"No way!" Wes moved over to block his brother from getting any closer to Marylin. "You're not supposed to be a part of this, Ty! You're not supposed to be kissing my guests! The bottle's pointing closer to me than anyone else, so I'll kiss Marylin!"

Wes leaned over to Marylin, his lips puckered. Marylin felt her throat tighten, and she was afraid she might start to cry at any second. She decided she didn't like this game very much. She wanted to choose whom she got to kiss. Other people shouldn't be able to choose for her.

Wes's lips pressed lightly against Marylin's mouth, and then it was over. Her second kiss. It was better than the first, but it wasn't the kiss she wanted.

"I can't believe you almost had to kiss Ty," Caitlin said after the party as she and Marylin walked to the car. "That would have been really horrible."

"It wouldn't have been so bad," Marylin said.

Caitlin looked at her with a shocked expression. "He's only got one leg, Marylin."

Marylin nodded. She knew that. She also knew that legs didn't have anything to do with kissing. In fact she was starting to think lips didn't have much to do with kissing either. Kissing was about hearts. She touched the glove in her coat pocket. As far as Marylin was concerned, she was still waiting for her first kiss.

hoop dreams

"Put your hands up, Kate! Play some defense!"

Kate narrowed her eyes and raised her hands over her head. She knew she couldn't outjump her dad, but maybe she could intimidate him into losing the ball.

"Yow-eeee!" Kate's yell bounced off the walls of the gym as her dad dribbled the ball down the court. He feigned left, then pivoted right. Kate charged him, slapping the ball away in mid-bounce. She turned, dribbled twice, then arched the ball into the air.

"She shoots! She scores! She is the champion of the world!"

"All right, Katie!" Kate's dad trotted over to her and they slapped high fives. All around them the gym echoed with the sound of basketballs hitting the wood floor and bouncing off backboards and rims. Most of the players were teenage boys and middle-aged men. Being around so many guys had made Kate feel shy when she'd first started coming to the gym with her dad to help him with his exercise-to-beat-stress program his doctor had put him on. But after a while she realized they were too busy playing ball to pay attention to her, so she stopped paying attention to them.

Kate's dad checked his watch. "It's almost eleven, which means Men's League practice is about to start," he said. "That's too bad, actually, because I was just about to make my big comeback."

"Says you," Kate said, tossing the basketball at her dad.

"Think fast, Kate," a voice called from behind her. She turned to see Andrew O'Shea lobbing a basketball in her direction. She caught it without even trying. Andrew was wearing baggy shorts like the ones the pros wore, and huge shoes that made the rest of his legs seem skinny as pencils. He looked completely different from the way he looked at school. At school Andrew usually wore tan pants and checkered shirts and deck shoes. Marcie Grossman said he dressed like his mom still picked out his clothes.

"Hey, Andrew," Kate greeted him when he walked over to where she and her dad were standing.

"Andrew?" Kate's dad whispered. "Who's this Andrew, huh?"

Kate shushed him. Then she turned to Andrew and said, "This is my dad. Don't pay attention to anything he says."

Kate's dad stuck out his hand for Andrew to shake. "Mel Faber," he said, introducing himself. "It's nice to meet you, Andrew. You here shooting some hoops with your dad?"

"Nah," Andrew said. "I'm here playing with my brothers." He pointed to a group of teenagers on the other side of the gym, two of whom had the same blond hair as Andrew and the same gold-framed glasses. "Except now they've got practice, so I'm just watching." He turned to Kate. "You could hang out and watch with me, if you want. We can give you a ride home later."

Kate looked at her dad, who shrugged and said, "It's up to you, sweetheart."

Kate hated it when her dad said stuff like "It's up to you, sweetheart." Didn't he know that parental guidance was necessary when it came to a girl her age watching basketball with a boy who was admittedly sort of cute but also goofy? A boy she had never thought about in a romantic way, but who might become a romantic prospect if she sat next to him in the gym? Did Kate even want a romantic prospect? She had no idea.

"Okay," Kate said finally, not knowing what else to say. "I guess I'll stay."

Kate followed Andrew over to the bleachers near where his brothers' team was practicing. *Maybe they'll notice me and ask me if I want to play,* she thought. *Maybe they'll put me on their team. Yeah, we know she's only eleven,* she could hear Andrew's brothers saying to the men's league officials. *But she's almost twelve, and she's got the best two-handed layup we've ever seen in our lives.*

"So what's this thing with you and Andrew O'Shea?" Marcie Grossman asked Kate in the bathroom after lunch on Monday. "Why do you guys keep looking at each other that way?"

"What way?" Kate asked. She could see

splotches of red blooming across her cheeks in the mirror.

"You know what way I mean!" Marcie said, punching Kate on the shoulder. "Like you're in love with each other or something."

Kate splashed some water on her face, then dried it off with a paper towel. "You're crazy, Marcie. Andrew and I are friends. We both like basketball."

"You both like each other! Wait until I tell everyone!"

"I don't care," Kate said. "You can tell people whatever you want. Go ahead. No one will believe you."

By two thirty-five that afternoon everyone in the sixth grade had heard that Kate and Andrew O'Shea were a couple.

"You should tell Andrew to get contacts," Flannery said, sliding into the seat next to Kate on the bus. "He might be cute if he didn't wear those stupid-looking glasses."

"Do you have to sit here?" Kate asked, looking straight ahead. "There are a thousand other places you could sit on this bus."

"It's a free country," Flannery replied in a singsong voice.

Kate glanced at Flannery out of the corner of her eye. At the beginning of April, Flannery had cut her hair as short as a boy's and dyed it red. It actually looked pretty good—not that Kate would ever tell Flannery that. She tried to say as little as possible to Flannery now that the only time she saw her was on the bus. After Marylin became a cheerleader, Flannery made friends with two eighth-grade girls who spent most of their time in the girls' room experimenting with lip gloss and purple eye shadow.

Flannery jabbed Kate with her elbow. "So have you kissed him yet?"

Kate glared at her. "That's none of your business!"

"That means yes!" Flannery crowed. "Kate, I never knew you were so mature!"

Kate ignored Flannery for the rest of the ride home. Of course she hadn't kissed Andrew! She didn't even know if she liked him. Okay, maybe she liked him a little. She liked talking to him, anyway. Saturday Kate and Andrew had watched basketball practice for two hours. They talked about school and how Mrs. Watson, their math and social studies teacher, should chew breath mints so that you didn't practically faint every time she breathed on you. They talked about how they missed Paisley Clark now that she was at a school for accelerated children, and discussed what Jason Frey could do to stop being so shy. Kate talked about her dad's heart attack last fall, and Andrew talked about his parents' divorce when he was seven. By the time basketball practice was over, Kate and Andrew had talked so much, their voices had grown ragged and raspy.

"Kissy-kissy," Flannery said to Kate as she got off the bus. "Don't let your lips get too chapped!"

When Kate stomped into her house a few minutes later, the phone was ringing. Melinda, the baby-sitter, picked it up. Turning to Kate, she whispered, "It's for you! It's a boy!"

"Give me that!" Kate said, grabbing the receiver from Melinda.

"Was that your mom?" Andrew O'Shea asked. Kate could tell it was him, although his voice sounded kind of funny over the phone.

"My baby-sitter," Kate told him. "She's nineteen going on eight."

Melinda made a pouty face at Kate from the kitchen table. Kate took the phone into the hall closet.

"So I hear we're an item," Andrew said. "Marcie Grossman has been telling everyone."

Kate felt her face grow hot. "I didn't say a

word to Marcie. Marcie just likes to make stuff up."

"Oh, I thought maybe you said something," Andrew said, sounding disappointed. "I mean, it's okay if you did."

"You wouldn't care?"

Andrew laughed. "Of course I wouldn't care! I think it's sort of neat. I mean, what do you think? About us, like, going together or something?"

"Or something?"

"About us going together," Andrew said more firmly. "I mean, do you want to?"

"Okay," Kate said, surprising herself with how quickly she answered. "I guess so. Sure."

"Great!" Andrew said.

"Great!" Kate replied.

Then neither of them said anything for a few minutes. Kate's legs started itching. Her stomach growled so loudly, she was sure Andrew could hear it. Finally she said, "Listen, the baby-sitter says I have to go clean my room. I'll talk to you tomorrow, okay?"

Then she walked out of the closet. Melinda beamed at her. "Is it true love?" she asked.

Kate didn't bother answering. Why everyone suddenly found her life so fascinating was beyond her.

When Kate got off the bus Tuesday morning, she saw Andrew getting off his bus at the other end of the drop-off lane. Panic grabbed her around the middle. It occurred to her that since she and Andrew were now officially going together, he might want to hold hands with her in front of everyone.

This idea terrified Kate so much that she ducked around the corner of the school before Andrew could see her and ran to the gym's back entrance. Inside, the before-school program kids were playing Hacky Sack and shooting baskets. Kate scooped up a ball from under the bleachers and dribbled over to where a handful of boys played a listless game of horse.

"You guys know how to play around the world?" Kate asked, twirling the ball expertly on her index finger.

Five minutes later, after Kate had circled the globe once and was halfway around again, Andrew walked into the gym. He smiled at Kate when he saw her but stopped for a minute to kick around the Hacky Sack with some seventh graders before ambling over.

"How about a game of one-on-one?" he asked casually.

Having a boyfriend's not so bad, Kate thought as she took the ball left, faking Andrew out, then shot neatly for an easy two points. For the next five minutes, until the bell rang, she and Andrew charged at each other, swiped the ball out of each other's hands, and tried long, impossible shots from half-court.

"Good game," Andrew said, patting Kate on the back as they walked from the gym to their first-period math class. "You ought to come over to my house one afternoon, and we can take on my brothers."

Kate was just about to agree to this when she looked up to see that she and Andrew were surrounded. Mrs. Watson hadn't unlocked her room yet, and all of Kate and Andrew's classmates were waiting outside the door, leaning against lockers and batting wads of paper at one another across the hall.

"Oooooh, look at the lovebirds," someone crooned. Immediately a whole chorus of *oooohs* started up. Kate saw Andrew's face grow red, but he smiled and shrugged his shoulders as though his classmates had caught him stealing from a cookie jar. She quickly walked over to where Marcie stood with Amber and Timma.

"You've got a big mouth," she said to Marcie.

"I wasn't saying anything that wasn't true," Marcie insisted. "You guys just proved it. Anyway, what's the big deal?"

Kate honestly didn't know. She looked to where Andrew was now standing with Jason Frey and Trevor Parlier. He really was halfway cute, she told herself, and he was a pretty good basketball player, even if he did have a bad habit of double dribbling when he got frustrated.

"Sorry I'm late, folks." Mrs. Watson walked through the crowd of kids, jangling her keys. Kate trailed Marcie and Amber into the classroom. She heard Mazie Calloway squeal, "Quit it, Robbie!" behind her.

Mazie Calloway would never want Andrew for a boyfriend—Kate knew that much. Neither would Ashley Greer or Ruby Santiago or Caitlin Moore. Or Marylin. None of the middle school cheerleaders ever had boyfriends whose moms still dressed them or who brought

Thermoses of milk to drink with their lunches instead of Cokes or sports drinks.

Maybe that was why it was such a big surprise when Marylin stopped by Kate's desk on her way down the aisle and said, "I think it's sort of cool about you and Andrew." She had a funny expression on her face. It wasn't until a few minutes later that Kate realized Marylin actually looked jealous, like she wished she had a boyfriend too. Marylin hadn't been jealous of Kate since fourth grade, when Kate had gotten a skateboard for her birthday. Marylin's mother was against skateboards for children.

Unfortunately a little envy from Marylin didn't change the fact that people would start expecting Kate to hold hands with Andrew in public. *Maybe I should tell my mom about Andrew*, she thought. Maybe she'll say, "You're much too young to have a boyfriend. Maybe when you're fourteen." *I'm sorry*, Kate would have to tell Andrew. *We can still play basketball, but only as friends.*

"He sounds like a nice boy. When do we get to meet him?"

Kate leaned back in her chair and let out a long sigh. This was not going as planned. Instead of giving her a firm lecture about being too young for boys, Kate's mom was calmly chopping up onions for dinner.

"What boy?" Tracie asked, walking into the kitchen and grabbing some grated cheddar cheese from the bowl by her mother's elbow. "Don't tell me Kate has a boyfriend. Who is it?"

"You wouldn't know him," Kate said. "His name is Andrew O'Shea. Besides, he's not really my boyfriend. He's more like a boy who's a friend."

"Is he related to Dave O'Shea?" Tracie asked.

Kate nodded. Dave was one of Andrew's older brothers.

"Geeksville!" Tracie said, hopping onto the stool next to the counter. "That whole family is from Mars. Dave O'Shea, Brian O'Shea, they're always winning these science contests, and all the teachers love them."

"Some people would say that that's a good thing, Tracie," Kate's mom said, reaching for a dish towel.

"They're really good basketball players," Kate said, defending Andrew's brothers.

Tracie laughed. "Who cares? They're geeks."

Later that night Kate sat on her bed and doodled in her social studies notebook. She was supposed to be brainstorming a list of the Ten Most Important Natural Resources of the Future, but she couldn't concentrate. The whole problem with love, Kate decided, was that it was the opposite of basketball. With basketball the object was simple: You put a round ball through a round hoop. You had to overcome some obstacles to score, sure, but if you practiced hard and played smart, you could win.

With love there was no ball and there was no hoop. And as far as Kate could tell, there was no winning. There was just Andrew O'Shea, a very nice person whose hand she didn't want to hold because she was afraid everyone would make fun of her. In the old days, when Kate had no interest in romance, she never cared what other people thought. Now, it appeared, love was turning her into a rotten human being.

Andrew was getting a drink at the water fountain outside the cafeteria. There was something about the way his neck showed so that Kate could see the top bump of his spine that made him look innocent to her, like he was a little kid who still believed in Santa Claus.

"Go ahead," she said, bumping Marcie with her hip. "Go talk to him!"

Kate quickly walked into the cafeteria and sat down with Amber and Timma. A few minutes later Marcie came over to the table.

"He said okay, no problem," she told Kate, throwing her lunch on the table.

"What happened?" Amber asked.

"Did you break up with Andrew?" Timma asked as she bit into her sandwich.

Kate shrugged. "It wasn't working out."

Kate was sure she had made the right decision until social studies, when Andrew read his list of the Top Ten Most Important Natural Resources of the Future. It was a really good list. For the tenth item he had put "Tiger Woods" and everyone had laughed, even Mrs. Watson, who usually didn't appreciate her students joking around on homework assignments.

Andrew looked straight ahead and didn't even glance at Kate as he passed her desk on the way back to his seat.

"I heard you dumped Andrew," Flannery

said from the seat behind Kate on the bus that afternoon.

"Why do you care so much about my life?" Kate asked, not bothering to turn around. "Why is what I do so important to you?"

"I don't care, actually," Flannery said, leaning forward and resting her elbows on the back of Kate's seat. "But I don't not care either. Watching what happens to you is like a scientific experiment."

"What am I?" Kate asked. "A lab rat?"

"Not exactly," Flannery said. "But you are interesting. You have a lot more potential than I thought you did. Which is more than I can say for Marylin."

The two girls were silent for a minute. Then Flannery sat up in her seat. "Anyway, it's too bad about Andrew. What happened anyway?"

Kate turned around and looked at Flannery. "It's too hard to explain. I can hardly explain it to myself."

Flannery nodded. "Love is a lot more complicated than people think."

Kate sat in the hallway closet and stared at the phone receiver. Then she looked up at the list of phone numbers she'd penciled on the closet wall in very tiny letters so that her mom wouldn't notice. Marylin's was on the very top, even though Kate had memorized Marylin's phone number a hundred million years ago. Under Marylin's name was a long list of names and numbers from the kids in her fifth-grade class. Kate had copied them from the school directory very carefully on the wall one night when her parents had gone out to dinner. At the time it had seemed like a good idea, although now it struck Kate as sort of dumb. She'd never called half those kids, and anyway she could have just looked them up in the phone book.

Her eyes tripped down to the bottom of the

list, where the sixth-grade names were, and found the number she'd been looking for. Kate smiled as she punched in the buttons.

"I think Andrew's great!" Paisley exclaimed after Kate had explained the situation to her. "But maybe you're not ready for love."

"How can you tell?" Kate wanted to know. "It seems like half the girls I know have boyfriends."

"But that doesn't mean they're ready for love," Paisley insisted. "Phoebe says that you should always start as friends first, anyway. Which you and Andrew did, but that still doesn't mean you have to be boyfriend and girlfriend."

"But maybe I want to be boyfriend and girlfriend." Kate sighed. "I wish it could all be private. Why does everybody have to know about everything in my life?"

Paisley laughed. "Why don't you quit thinking about love and boyfriends and girlfriends?

Why don't you just think about Andrew O'Shea, the human being?"

Kate stretched her legs so that they were poking out into the hallway and examined her shoes, which had extra-bouncy soles so she could jump extra high. Andrew had a pair just like them. Andrew the human being.

"Maybe I'll try that," she told Paisley. "But sometimes it's hard to think about other people as human beings. Too much stuff gets in the way."

Then she and Paisley decided to do their homework on the phone together, and Kate actually helped Paisley with a math problem, which made Kate feel like maybe she could be an accelerated child, and they talked about some things they might do that summer, like hang out at a creek that was near Kate's house and famous for its frogs. For forty-five minutes, until Tracie started yelling at Kate to quit yakking and let someone else talk on the phone for a change, Kate forgot all about boys and love and caring what other people thought about her. She was too busy thinking about how nice it was to have friends like Paisley.

And, it occurred to her all of a sudden, like Andrew O'Shea.

As soon as she walked into the gym before school the next morning, Kate saw Andrew shooting baskets with a couple of guys from Mr. Tower's homeroom. She almost turned around, but she stopped herself. She wasn't going to spend the rest of her life trying to avoid Andrew O'Shea. She'd hardly ever get a chance to play basketball if she did that.

It's time to set things straight, Kate thought. The least she could do was talk to him in person, instead of sending her friends to do her dirty work.

Kate ran across the court from Andrew,

holding up her hands. "I've got an open shot!" she called to him. "Throw it here."

Looking confused, Andrew lobbed the ball at Kate. She grabbed it, then put it into the air. The ball teetered on the rim for a few seconds before falling through the net.

"Two on two!" Tim Lopez, one of the guys from Mr. Tower's homeroom, called out. "Me and Charlie versus Kate and Andrew. No competition!"

Kate took the ball back to half-court, then passed it off to Andrew, who made an easy layup. For the next five minutes they played like they'd been on the same team all their lives. Finally Tim held up his hands as if he were surrendering.

"I've got to go get my books before the bell."

"Yeah, me too," Charlie said, scurrying after Tim out of the gym.

"Amateurs," Kate said to Andrew, throwing him the ball. "Tim should stick to soccer."

"Yeah," Andrew agreed. "He's a lot better with his feet than his hands."

Kate kicked the floor with the toe of her shoe. "So anyway," she said, "when are we going to play against your brothers?"

"I thought you didn't want to do stuff with me anymore," Andrew said, looking closely at the basketball as though he were inspecting it for very tiny holes.

Kate took the ball from him and put it on top of her head. "It's not that," she said, moving her neck and shoulders around to keep the ball balanced. "It's just that I don't want to hold hands. I don't think I'm any good at holding hands."

"Probably because you're too busy using them to play defense," Andrew said, grabbing the ball off Kate's head and dribbling it toward the hoop. Kate ran after him, putting her hands up to block his shot. But instead of stealing the ball away from Andrew when she had a chance, she grabbed his wrist.

"Maybe I could start with wrists and work my way down to hands," she told him, suddenly inspired. "Maybe that would be okay."

Andrew smiled. Then he hooked the ball into the air with his free hand. Kate watched as it curved neatly into the basket, falling through the net without a sound.

A bunch of kids who'd been watching them play cheered and stomped their feet. Kate let her hand slip into Andrew's for just a second, and then she went for the rebound. She put her hands up. She opened her arms.

One day Petey McIntosh is going to write a book on how to be a household spy. At the age of nine he is already an expert. His favorite spying method is to put his ear to the heating duct on his bedroom floor and listen very carefully for voices coming through the vents. This is how he knows his parents are getting a divorce. His sister, Marylin, has no idea.

Of course, the sun could go supernova and Marylin wouldn't notice. She'd be too busy writing the name of her latest boyfriend over and over with a purple pen in her diary to pay attention to something as inconsequential as the end of the world.

Petey's second favorite spying method is reading things he has no business reading, such as Marylin's diary. The most interesting thing about Marylin's diary is that she sometimes writes in code. Yesterday, for instance, she wrote "RBIAC" seventeen times. Petey sits in front of the TV pretending to watch *Mighty Monster Brigade* when in fact he is trying to figure out what "RBIAC" means. Pretending to do one thing while he's actually doing another is a spy technique that has served Petey well over the years. Who would guess that at this very minute he is composing a list in his head that goes:

Red Baboons In Alligator Coats
Really Big Iguanas All Colors
Run Battery In Air Conditioner

"Petey, come set the table, please!"

Petey considers acting like he hasn't heard

his mom call him from the kitchen, but then he remembers about the divorce and thinks he ought not to make her life any harder than it already is. Besides, it's possible that his mom knows something about "RBIAC." Ever since Marylin "forgot" to show her parents her report card last month, his mom sometimes makes random checks of Marylin's backpack, in case there are any D– math tests lurking in there. Maybe his mom has run across some clues to the "RBIAC" mystery beneath Marylin's gym socks and social studies reports.

"Is Dad coming home for dinner?" Petey asks his mom as he takes the silverware from its drawer.

"He's got a meeting, sweetie," his mom says. "But Mazie's coming home with Marylin after cheerleading, so set the usual number of places."

Petey groans. Mazie Calloway has been Marylin's best friend ever since they both made the middle school cheerleading squad in February. Every other word she says is "like" or "you know," and she acts like Petey is the family pet instead of an actual person. Petey misses Marylin's old best friend, Kate, who was always up for a game of make it, take it if Petey could find the pump to blow up his basketball.

"Hey, Mom," Petey calls from the dining room, where he is carefully laying out the forks and knives. "Read Books In American Culture!"

"Excuse me, sweetie? I didn't quite hear what you were saying," his mom calls back.

Petey tries again. "Reckon Bears Insure All Caves?"

Petey's mom walks into the dining room. "Either I'm losing my hearing, or else you're not making any sense."

"Really? Been In A Car Wreck?"

"Of course I haven't been in a car wreck!"

his mom says. She is starting to sound a little bit irritated.

"Rings Bells If Almost Close," Petey offers.

Petey's mom shakes her head. "I really don't understand the male of my species," she says. "I thought I did once, but I must have been mistaken."

"It's not nice to generalize," Petey tells her, repeating one of his mom's favorite sayings.

Try understanding girls is what he says to himself as he straightens out the place mats. Just try it. And then he realizes that that is exactly what he is attempting to do. RBIAC. It is some secret girl code, he's sure of it, and he is just the man to figure it out.

"Like, Mrs. Watson is, you know, a witch!"

Mazie Calloway is chatting to Marylin's mother through a mouthful of vegetarian pizza. Marylin has thought about telling Mazie privately that she should chew with her mouth closed and swallow her food before she speaks, but she doesn't. Marylin is afraid that Mazie will turn around and tell her something she does that's totally gross. What if Marylin sticks her pinkie in her ear and searches around for earwax when they have free reading in language arts period? Marylin sometimes catches herself doing this at night when she's writing in her diary. If she does it at school, she's not sure that she wants to know.

Marylin hates to be told anything bad about herself. She hates reading the slam books that circulate through her sixth-grade class, even though most people write nice things about her, like "Cute!" and "A good friend" and "Not stuck-up for a cheerleader." Once someone wrote, "She's okay," and Marylin felt like she'd been slapped. Why didn't this anonymous person think she was wonderful or at least nice? She'd nearly worn out her lips smiling at everyone, even Matthew Sholls, for weeks afterward, just to prove that she was more than "okay."

"Our new cheerleading uniforms are so cute, Mrs. McIntosh," Mazie chatters on. "Are you going to come to the soccer game Friday afternoon? Because we have, like, this really cute new cheer we're going to do."

Mazie has a reputation for being good with parents and teachers. It's because she's perky, Marylin thinks. Parents and teachers think if you're perky on the outside, you must be sweet and good on the inside. This is where Mazie has grown-ups fooled.

"Let's humiliate someone," Mazie says after dinner, when she and Marylin are lying on Marylin's blue carpet with their feet planted against the wall.

"Who do you want to humiliate?" Marylin asks. She supposes she should ask why Mazie wants to humiliate someone, but Mazie would probably take it the wrong way and end up trying to humiliate Marylin.

"How about Kate Faber?" Mazie suggests. "I know you used to be sort of friends with her, but she's so weird, you know? And she has fat knees."

"Really?" Marylin has known Kate since nursery school and has never noticed that she has fat knees. Kate is actually a very muscular person, in Marylin's opinion. Marylin looks at her own knees. They're sort of knobby, but you wouldn't call them fat.

"Like, amazingly fat knees," Mazie says. "It makes me sick to look at them."

The problem with being friends with Mazie, Marylin has discovered, is that she spends a lot of time wishing she were five years old again. Marylin has fond memories of being five, like eating cinnamon toast while she watched cartoons on Saturday morning. She doesn't remember ever paying attention to people's knees or feeling like she was always on the verge of doing something terrible.

Mazie turns over on her side and props her head up with her elbow. "I was thinking we could get Robbie Ballard to write Kate a note that says, like, 'Dear Kate, Do you want to go to the movies with me Friday?' or something. 'Check yes or no.' Of course she'll check 'Yes,' and then Robbie will tell her it's a big joke."

"I don't know, Mazie," Marylin says, stalling. "I think Kate sort of has a boyfriend. You know, Andrew O'Shea?" Marylin isn't sure about this, because she never sees Kate and Andrew holding hands on the playground. But they spend a lot of time together, and sometimes Marylin catches Andrew and Kate smiling at each other in a secret sort of way, like they know something that no one else does. She would love to call Kate up and ask her what's going on, but she doesn't think Kate would tell her.

"Andrew O'Shea!" Mazie laughs. "Believe me, even if she's engaged to be married to Andrew O'Shea, she wouldn't turn down a chance to go to the movies with Robbie."

Marylin scrambles for another excuse not to do this thing to Kate. "Robbie wouldn't be able to keep a straight face. Kate would know something was up, even before she read the note."

Mazie considers this. "Okay," she says after a moment. "Kate lives down the street from you, right? So, you know, you can slip the note in her mailbox Saturday morning. That'll give her all weekend to get excited about it, and then Monday morning, *wham!* The joke's on her."

If her life were a TV show, this is where Marylin would stand up and say, *No, that's a horrible thing to do to someone! Kate Faber is a very nice person. One time she stayed up all night feeding a baby bird whose mom had died. And her mom always made chocolate-chip cookies when I spent the night at their house, so I am not going to do this really mean thing to her!*

Unfortunately Marylin's life is just her life. On one side of it is Mazie and cheerleading and being invited to boy-girl parties that she's only invited to because of Mazie and cheerleading. On the other side is Kate. Marylin sighs. She knows which side she has chosen, even if sometimes her choice makes her stomach hurt.

"Okay," she tells Mazie. "If you really think Robbie will write the note."

Mazie giggles. "Of course Robbie will write the note. He's in love with me, isn't he?"

Of course.

Petey rolls away from the heating duct and rubs his ear. So RB is Robbie Ballard, and Robbie Ballard is in love with Mazie, not Marylin. Maybe IAC stands for Is A Chucklehead.

The whole thing reminds Petey of a soap opera. Whenever Petey stays home sick from school, he watches soap operas in the afternoon, not because he likes them, but because other people like them. To be a good spy, Petey knows, you have to understand what makes human beings tick, and that means figuring out why they like the things they like and hate the things they hate. So far Petey hasn't figured out why some people like soap operas. For one thing, there's way too much kissing.

Petey gets up and walks over to his desk. He does his best thinking sitting on his hardback chair and staring at his poster of Albert Einstein. Albert Einstein would probably have made a great spy, if he hadn't been so busy coming up with theories of time and space.

Petey knows that as a spy his job is to observe, not to act. But what he has just learned calls for action. He leans back in his chair. He will come up with a plan. Good will triumph over evil, if Petey McIntosh has anything to do with it.

Kate is pretending to watch a video on Saturday morning, but really she is staring at her knees. She is worried that they're fat.

Her mom keeps telling her that she's not the least bit fat, but that's what moms get paid to say. It's bad enough Kate has bone-straight, plain-brown hair and a bad habit of biting her cuticles. The last thing she needs is fat knees.

Maybe she can find some knee exercises in one of the magazines Tracie has piled beneath her bed. Tracie has six magazine subscriptions and knows everything there is to know about makeup and exercises to improve your figure. Sometimes Kate picks up one of Tracie's magazines and tries to read it, but she doesn't get the articles. What is an eyelash curler? And why would anyone wash her hair with eggs and rinse it out with vinegar?

Well, Kate decides, there's no use crying over fat knees. She finds her basketball and goes out to the driveway to practice her layups. Kate's dream is that one day they will let girls play in the NBA. She plans to be the first girl NBA player with a multimillion dollar contract to endorse tennis shoes. She has already planned what she will say in her commercial.

"Hi there, folks, I'm Kate Faber, basketball champion. You know, when I was a kid, I could have been a cheerleader, but I decided to play basketball instead. Now I'm a famous million-aire! So wear Zippo shoes and be a star, just like me!"

Kate hopes Marylin will see her commercial and feel terrible. Or else call her and say, "Kate, I'm really sorry about what happened in sixth grade. Can we be friends again?"

In Kate's imagination the phone makes a satisfying click when she hangs up without saying a word.

Outside, Kate's street is empty, and the hollow ring of the basketball against the pavement startles the birds from the tree in her front yard. Kate lunges toward the basket, pushes off on her left leg, and angles the ball against the backboard for an easy two points. The roar of the crowd echoes inside her head. Kate makes a bow to the azalea bush.

"Thank you," she says graciously. "Michael Jordan taught me everything I know."

She glances toward Marylin's house and wonders if she might be watching from her window. Not that Kate cares. She wouldn't be friends with Marylin again for all the shoe endorsements in the world. Any person who considers Mazie Calloway her best friend is not worth the time of day, in Kate's opinion. It is a shame that Marylin grew up to be such a shallow person, but there's nothing Kate can do about it now except forget Marylin ever existed.

The weird thing is, Kate is pretty sure she saw Marylin in front of her house this morning. But by the time Kate opened the front door and looked out, no one was there. Now she wonders if she dreamed it. Kate did a report about dreams for school a few weeks ago, and she learned that dreams are the language of the subconscious. Sometimes Kate wishes her subconscious would just shut up.

"Hey, Kate, want to play make it, take it?"

Kate turns around to see Petey McIntosh leaning his bike against her mailbox. He appears to be stuffing something white into his jacket pocket, but Kate can't tell what it is.

"Sure, Petey," she says. "If you think you're up to the competition."

"You better believe it, babe," Petey says as he walks down the driveway.

Kate puts the ball into the air and watches it sail through the hoop without touching the rim.

"So what's Marylin doing today?" she asks casually as she retrieves the ball. Not that she cares. Later she has plans to play basketball with Andrew, and tomorrow she and Paisley are going to the movies. Frankly,

Kate doesn't need Marylin McIntosh in her life.

Petey shrugs. "Stupid stuff. Mazie Calloway is teaching her how to use an eyelash curler. It's pretty weird."

"Yeah, that's weird all right," Kate says. She shoots again and this time misses the basket completely.

"Marylin, I need to talk to you."

Marylin looks up from the hand mirror she's been staring in. Is her mother mad at her for using an eyelash curler?

"An eyelash curler isn't makeup, Mom, okay? You never said anything about me not trying to make my eyelashes look longer."

Marylin's mother sits down next to her on the couch. Marylin wishes Mazie had stayed for lunch. Her mother never yells at her when she has company.

"I don't care about your eyelashes," her mom says.

"Then can I wear mascara?"

Marylin's mom lets out a small groan. "Marylin, this is important!"

Kate got the note and figured out our plan. Kate's mom called my mom. I'm doomed, Marylin thinks.

"It's just a joke, Mom," she says, defending herself.

"What's just a joke?" her mom asks. "You know, Marylin, sometimes I think we don't speak the same language anymore."

"Habla Español?" Marylin giggles.

Later Marylin sits on her bed and tries to write in her diary. She uses a black pen because her purple pen doesn't seem right for what she has to say. Then she discovers she has no words for what she has to say.

"MPAGAD," she writes. "My parents are getting a—." But she can't even think it. And there's no one she can say it out loud to. How in the world could she call up Mazie Calloway and tell her? You have to be careful what you say to Mazie, Marylin has learned over the past few months. When Marylin told Mazie that Mr. Kertzner and Aunt Tish were engaged, Mazie spread it all through the sixth grade, like they were doing something incredibly weird. Just think what Mazie would do if Marylin told her about her parents.

Suddenly she thinks of Kate, but Marylin can't talk to Kate, can she? What would she say? Sorry about not really being your friend anymore, but would you mind if I told you all my problems now that I need you? Kate would probably laugh and hang up on her. Just imagining the receiver's click in her ear makes Marylin want to cry.

She stands up. "I'm going to wash my hair," she tells Zuzu, her stuffed panda. "Do you think my eyelashes will stay curly in the shower?"

But Marylin doesn't wash her hair. Instead she pulls on a sweater and heads toward Kate's house. Even though the air is cool, Marylin feels hot, as though someone has set tiny fires all over her skin. She walks along the edges of the flowerbeds she passes, hoping to tempt people to come out of their houses and yell at her. She would like to have an excuse to hit someone.

Kate's house looks the way it has always looked, which surprises Marylin. The last few months she has pictured it with the shutters falling off their hinges and the lawn overgrown with weeds, as though the Fabers wouldn't bother taking care of things now that Marylin has stopped coming over.

When she opens the Fabers' mailbox, after looking around to make sure no one sees her, it's empty.

"Marylin, sweetheart!" Kate's mom opens the front door. "Come on in and have some cookies! I just pulled a fresh batch from the oven! I'm in one of my baking sprees. I must have sensed you were coming over."

"I can't!" Marylin yells. "But tell Kate it's a joke!"

Mrs. Faber looks confused. "What's a joke, sweetheart?"

"Just give her that message, please! Just tell her it's a joke and not to say anything on Monday!"

Marylin reels around and runs, crashing against shrubbery and nearly tripping on a clump of weeds growing out of a crack in the sidewalk. When she gets to her house, she doesn't slow down. She runs like she is being chased by the scariest thing in the world.

Monday morning Petey arranges his books alphabetically in his backpack, then checks the front pocket to make sure all his spying tools are in place. At all times Petey carries a magnifying glass, a tiny tape recorder, a compass, a small notebook to record his observations in, and a folded sheet of paper with Morse code copied on it, in case he's ever captured by the enemy.

Petey slips the note intended for Kate Faber between the tape recorder and the magnifying glass. Who knows—it might come in handy someday. He has thought about showing it to Gretchen Humboldt, his science partner, to see if she can explain it to him. Petey knows what the note says, but he has no idea why Marylin and Mazie thought it would be funny to give it to Kate. *Fooling with the human heart is no laughing matter,* he might say to Gretchen.

After Petey finishes checking his backpack, he leans down next to the heating duct and presses his ear against it. Usually when he does this in the morning, all he hears is the wheeze and shudder of the coffee maker. But today the voices of Marylin and his mom flow up through the vent.

"I'm really not in the mood for school today, Mom," Marylin says. "I just can't go."

"Are you sick?"

Marylin sniffles. "No, I just feel lousy after what we talked about Saturday."

Petey leans back on his haunches. What did Marylin and his mom talk about? How in the world did he miss out on this conversation?

"It's understandable you feel bad," his mom says. "But maybe you'll feel better if you go to school."

Feel bad about what? Petey wishes Marylin and his mom would quit circling around the subject and say what they mean.

"Going to school would just make me feel worse."

It comes to Petey in a flash. Marylin must have told his mom about the note on Saturday.

He can't believe it. Marylin actually feels bad about playing such a rotten trick on Kate. Petey is impressed.

Petey stands up and turns to look at his Albert Einstein poster. Einstein looks back at him with his gentle eyes. *Be kind,* he seems to be telling Petey. *Take pity on your sister.*

Rounding the corner into the kitchen, Petey grabs Marylin by the shoulder.

"Come here a second," he says to her, nodding toward the dining room. "I want to show you something."

"I'm not in the mood, Petey," Marylin says.

"It's important! It'll just take a second," Petey tells her.

Marylin follows Petey into the dining room, where Petey unzips his backpack pocket and takes out the note.

"She never got it," he whispers. "I grabbed it out of her mailbox before anyone found it."

Marylin's expression is a tangle of confusion. "What? But how? Who told you?"

Petey shrugs. "I know about a lot of things," he says, trying to sound mysterious.

Marylin takes the note from his hand. "She never saw it?"

"Nope," Petey says proudly.

"I don't know whether to thank you or sock you in the nose."

Petey puts his hands in front of his face. "Whatever you do, just don't kiss me," he says.

"Marylin," his mom calls, "I really think you should go to school."

"I told you, Mom, I feel too horrible about everything to go to school," Marylin calls back.

"But Kate didn't get the note," Petey whispers at her. "Remember?"

Marylin gives him a strange look. "What does that have to do with anything?"

Petey shakes his head.

Women.

Robbie Ballard has been hanging around Kate's desk all morning, throwing her hundred-watt smiles every time Kate looks in his direction. Given that Robbie Ballard has not spoken two words to her since third grade except to insult her, Kate finds these smiles of his a little unnerving.

Mazie Calloway has been smiling at her a lot too, Kate realizes. She looks down at her shirt. Did she spill grape juice on it this morning at breakfast? No, her shirt is stain free. It must be her fat knees, Kate decides. They can see her fat knees through her jeans.

When Mrs. Watson leaves the room to run an errand, Robbie Ballard pulls his desk closer to Kate's.

"So?" he asks, raising his eyebrows.

"So what?" Kate replies uneasily.

Robbie lets out a little laugh. "You know!"

Kate stares at him. This has got to be the weirdest moment of her life. She is apparently having a conversation with Robbie Ballard, but she has no idea what they're talking about.

"Come on, Kate!" Robbie exclaims. "What do you say?"

Tell her it's a joke, Marylin had told Kate's mom. *Tell her not to say anything Monday.*

Kate raises her eyebrows at Robbie but doesn't say a word.

"You know what I mean, Kate!" Robbie says. "The movies? Didn't you read the note?"

What note? Kate almost asks, but she stops herself. "What about it?"

Robbie shakes his head. "What do you mean, 'What about it?' Do you want to go to the movies or what?"

Kate smiles her own hundred-watt smile. "Nope," she says pleasantly.

"You don't want to go to the movies with me?" Robbie's mouth hangs open like he has just been socked in the guts.

"No thanks," Kate says, opening her math book and pretending to be absorbed in her fractions homework.

A buzz seems to follow Kate for the rest of the day. Everywhere she turns, people are looking at her as though they've never seen her before. At lunch Caitlin Moore hands her a slam book. "Sign this, okay, Kate? I just started it today."

Kate nods. As soon as Caitlin walks away, she turns to her page. She expects to find the usual column of "She's okay" beneath her name, but to Kate's surprise someone has written "Cute," and beneath that, in different handwriting, "Mysterious. Wish I knew her better."

Kate leans back in her chair and looks around the cafeteria. Smiles sparkle at her like flashbulbs from all over the room.

This is definitely the weirdest day of my life, Kate decides. She wishes someone would explain why she's such a star all of a sudden. She wishes she could still talk to Marylin. But what would she say?

When the phone rings that afternoon, Kate answers, "Hello?"

And then, "Hey, Marylin."

As it turns out, she knows exactly what to say.